"Are you having a g[...] W9-ASX-495

I am now. Stefan did[...] it was what he was thinking. She could see it in the way he stared at her. She had never been so sure of her power. Except that actually he didn't look as if he were having a good time; he looked stricken, in pain, as if he couldn't take one more minute of this.

The band was starting up, a slow dance. He was still staring at her, drinking her in. Those green eyes darkening, going black with desire. She had the sudden feeling that he might jerk her to him and kiss her hard, without ever saying a word.

"Would you like to dance?" she said softly. *I'm playing with fire, with something I don't understand,* she thought suddenly. And in that instant she realized that she was frightened. Her heart began to pound violently. It was as if those green eyes spoke to some part of her that was buried deep beneath the surface—and that part was screaming "danger" at her. Some instinct older than civilization was telling her to run, to flee.

She didn't move.

BOOKS BY L.J. SMITH

THE VAMPIRE DIARIES

Volume I: *The Awakening*
Volume II: *The Struggle*
Volume III: *The Fury*
Volume IV: *Dark Reunion*

THE SECRET CIRCLE TRILOGY

Volume I: *The Initiation*
Volume II: *The Captive*
Volume III: *The Power*

The Night of the Solstice
Heart of Valor

Published by HarperPaperbacks

ATTENTION: ORGANIZATIONS AND CORPORATIONS

Most HarperPaperbacks are available at special quantity discounts for bulk purchases for sales promotions, premiums, or fund-raising. For information, please call or write:
Special Markets Department, HarperCollins Publishers,
10 East 53rd Street, New York, N.Y. 10022.
Telephone: (212) 207-7528. Fax: (212) 207-7222.

The Awakening
Volume 1

L. J. Smith

HarperPrism

A Division of HarperCollins*Publishers*

■ HarperPrism
A Division of HarperCollins*Publishers*
10 East 53rd Street, New York, NY 10022–5299

This is a work of fiction. The characters, incidents,
and dialogues are products of the author's imagination and
are not to be construed as real. Any resemblance to actual events
or persons, living or dead, is entirely coincidental.

A mass market edition of this book was
published in 1991 by HarperPaperbacks.

Produced by Daniel Weiss Associates, Inc.,
33 West 17th Street, New York, NY 10011.

HarperPrism printing: March 1999

Printed in the United States of America

ISBN 0-06-102000-1

Visit HarperPrism on the World Wide Web at
http://www.harpercollins.com

❖ 10 9 8 7 6 5 4 3 2

The Awakening

One

September 4
Dear Diary,
~~Something awful is going to happen today.~~

I don't know why I wrote that. It's crazy. There's no reason for me to be upset and every reason for me to be happy, but . . .

But here I am at 5:30 in the morning, awake and scared. I keep telling myself it's just that I'm all messed up from the time difference between France and here. But that doesn't explain why I feel so scared. So lost.

The day before yesterday, while Aunt Judith and Margaret and I were driving back from the airport, I had such a strange feeling. When we turned onto our street I suddenly thought, "Mom and Dad are waiting for us at home. I bet they'll be on the front porch or in the living room looking out the window. They must have missed me so much."

1

I know. That sounds totally crazy.

But even when I saw the house and the empty front porch I still felt that way. I ran up the steps and I tried the door and knocked with the knocker. And when Aunt Judith unlocked the door I burst inside and just stood in the hallway listening, expecting to hear Mom coming down the stairs or Dad calling from the den.

Just then Aunt Judith let a suitcase crash down on the floor behind me and sighed a huge sigh and said, "We're home." And Margaret laughed. And the most horrible feeling I've ever felt in my life came over me. I've never felt so utterly and completely lost.

Home. I'm home. Why does that sound like a lie?

I was born here in Fell's Church. I've always lived in this house, always. This is my same old bedroom, with the scorch mark on the floorboards where Caroline and I tried to sneak cigarettes in 5th grade and nearly choked ourselves. I can look out the window and see the big quince tree Matt and the guys climbed up to crash my birthday slumber party two years ago. This is my bed, my chair, my dresser.

But right now everything looks strange to me, as if I don't belong here. It's me that's out of place. And the worst thing is that I feel there's somewhere I do belong, but I just can't find it.

I was too tired yesterday to go to Orientation.

Meredith picked up my schedule for me, but I didn't feel like talking to her on the phone. Aunt Judith told everyone who called that I had jet lag and was sleeping, but she watched me at dinner with a funny look on her face.

I've got to see the crowd today, though. We're supposed to meet in the parking lot before school. Is that why I'm scared? Am I frightened of them?

Elena Gilbert stopped writing. She stared at the last line she had written and then shook her head, pen hovering over the small book with the blue velvet cover. Then, with a sudden gesture, she lifted her head and threw pen and book at the big bay window, where they bounced off harmlessly and landed on the upholstered window seat.

It was all so completely ridiculous.

Since when had she, Elena Gilbert, been scared of meeting people? Since when had she been scared of *anything*? She stood up and angrily thrust her arms into a red silk kimono. She didn't even glance at the elaborate Victorian mirror above the cherrywood dresser; she knew what she'd see. Elena Gilbert, cool and blond and slender, the fashion trendsetter, the high school senior, the girl every boy wanted and every girl wanted to be. Who just now had an

3

unaccustomed scowl on her face and a pinch to her mouth.

A hot bath and some coffee and I'll calm down, she thought. The morning ritual of washing and dressing was soothing, and she dawdled over it, sorting through her new outfits from Paris. She finally chose a pale rose top and white linen shorts combo that made her look like a raspberry sundae. Good enough to eat, she thought, and the mirror showed a girl with a secret smile. Her earlier fears had melted away, forgotten.

"Elena! Where are you? You're going to be late for school!" The voice drifted faintly up from below.

Elena ran the brush one more time through silky hair and pulled it back with a deep rose ribbon. Then she grabbed her backpack and went down the stairs.

In the kitchen, four-year-old Margaret was eating cereal at the kitchen table, and Aunt Judith was burning something on the stove. Aunt Judith was the sort of woman who always looked vaguely flustered; she had a thin, mild face and light flyaway hair pushed back untidily. Elena landed a peck on her cheek.

"Good morning, everybody. Sorry I don't have time for breakfast."

"But, Elena, you can't just go off without eating. You need your protein—"

"I'll get a doughnut before school," said Elena briskly. She dropped a kiss on Margaret's tow head and turned to go.

"But, Elena—"

"And I'll probably go home with Bonnie or Meredith after school, so don't wait dinner. Bye!"

"Elena—"

Elena was already at the front door. She closed it behind her, cutting off Aunt Judith's distant protests, and stepped out onto the front porch.

And stopped.

All the bad feelings of the morning rushed over her again. The anxiety, the fear. And the certainty that something terrible was about to happen.

Maple Street was deserted. The tall Victorian houses looked strange and silent, as if they might all be empty inside, like the houses on an abandoned movie set. They looked as if they were empty of *people*, but full of strange watching things.

That was it; something was watching her. The sky overhead was not blue but milky and opaque, like a giant bowl turned upside down.

The air was stifling, and Elena felt sure that there were eyes on her.

She caught sight of something dark in the branches of the old quince tree in front of the house.

It was a crow, sitting as still as the yellow-tinged leaves around it. And it was the thing watching her.

She tried to tell herself that this was ridiculous, but somehow she *knew.* It was the biggest crow she had ever seen, plump and sleek, with rainbows shining in its black feathers. She could see every detail of it clearly: the greedy dark claws, the sharp beak, the single glittering black eye.

It was so motionless that it might have been a wax model of a bird sitting there. But as she stared at it, Elena felt herself flush slowly, heat coming in waves up her throat and cheeks. Because it was . . . looking at her. Looking the way boys looked at her when she wore a bathing suit or a sheer blouse. As if it were undressing her with its eyes.

Before she realized what she was doing, she had dropped her backpack and picked up a stone from beside the driveway. "Get out of here," she said, and heard the shaking anger in her own voice. "Go on! Get *away!*" With the last word, she threw the stone.

There was an explosion of leaves, but the crow soared up unharmed. Its wings were huge, and they made enough racket for a whole flock of crows. Elena crouched, suddenly panicked as it flapped directly over her head, the wind of its wings ruffling her blond hair.

But it swooped up again and circled, a black silhouette against the paper-white sky. Then, with one harsh croak, it wheeled away toward the woods.

Elena straightened up slowly, then glanced around, self-conscious. She couldn't believe what she had just done. But now that the bird was gone, the sky felt ordinary again. A little wind made the leaves flutter, and Elena took a deep breath. Down the street a door opened and several children poured out, laughing.

She smiled at them, and took another breath, relief sweeping through her like sunlight. How could she have been so silly? This was a beautiful day, full of promise, and nothing bad was going to happen.

Nothing bad was going to happen—except that she was going to be late getting to school. The whole crowd would be waiting for her in the parking lot.

You could always tell everyone you stopped to throw stones at a Peeping Tom, she thought, and almost giggled. Now, *that* would give them something to think about.

Without a backward glance at the quince tree, she began to walk as quickly as she could down the street.

The crow crashed through the top of the massive oak, and Stefan's head jerked up reflexively. When he saw it was only a bird, he relaxed.

His eyes dropped to the limp white form in his hands, and he felt his face twist in regret. He hadn't meant to kill it. He would have hunted something larger than a rabbit if he'd known how hungry he was. But, of course, that was the very thing that frightened him: never knowing how strong the hunger would be, or what he might have to do to satisfy it. He was lucky that this time he'd killed only a rabbit.

He stood beneath the ancient oak trees, sunlight filtering down onto his curly hair. In jeans and T-shirt, Stefan Salvatore looked exactly like a normal high school student.

He wasn't.

Deep in the woods, where no one would see him, he'd come to feed. Now he licked at his gums and lips painstakingly, to make sure there was no stain on them. He didn't want to take any chances. This masquerade was going to be hard enough to pull off as it was.

For a moment he wondered, again, if he should just give it all up. Perhaps he should go back to Italy, back to his hiding place. What made him think that he could rejoin the world of daylight?

But he was tired of living in shadows. He was tired of the darkness, and of the things that lived in it. Most of all, he was tired of being alone.

He wasn't sure why he'd chosen Fell's Church, Virginia. It was a young town, by his standards; the oldest buildings had been put up only a century and a half ago. But memories and ghosts of the Civil War still lived here, as real as the supermarkets and fast-food joints.

Stefan appreciated respect for the past. He thought he might come to like the people of Fell's Church. And perhaps—just perhaps—he might find a place among them.

He'd never be accepted completely, of course. A bitter smile curved his lips at the idea. He knew better than to hope for *that.* There would never be a place where he could belong completely, where he could truly be himself.

Unless he chose to belong to the shadows . . .

He slapped the thought away. He'd renounced the darkness; he'd left the shadows behind him. He was blotting all those long years out and starting afresh, today.

Stefan realized he was still holding the rabbit. Gently, he laid it down on the bed of brown oak leaves. Far away, too far for human ears to pick up, he recognized the noises of a fox.

Come along, brother hunter, he thought sadly. Your breakfast is waiting.

As he slung his jacket over his shoulder, he noticed the crow that had disturbed him earlier. It was still perched in the oak tree, and it seemed to be watching him. There was a wrongness about it.

He started to send a probing thought toward it, to examine the bird, and stopped himself. Remember your promise, he thought. You don't use the Powers unless it is absolutely necessary. Not unless there is no other choice.

Moving almost silently among the dead leaves and dry twigs, he made his way toward the edge of the woods. His car was parked there. He glanced back, once, and saw that the crow had left the branches and dropped down on the rabbit.

There was something sinister in the way it spread its wings over the limp white body, something sinister and triumphant. Stefan's throat tightened, and he almost strode back to chase the bird away. Still, it had as much right to eat as the fox did, he told himself.

As much right as he did.

If he encountered the bird again, he'd look into its mind, he decided. Just now, he tore his eyes from the sight of it and hurried on through the woods, jaw set. He didn't want to be late arriving at Robert E. Lee High School.

Two

Elena was surrounded the instant she stepped into the high school parking lot. Everyone was there, the whole crowd she hadn't seen since late June, plus four or five hangers-on who hoped to gain popularity by association. One by one she accepted the welcoming hugs of her own group.

Caroline had grown at least an inch and was slinkier and more like a *Vogue* model than ever. She greeted Elena coolly and stepped back again with her green eyes narrowed like a cat's.

Bonnie hadn't grown at all, and her curly red head barely came up to Elena's chin as she flung her arms around Elena. Wait a minute—*curls?* thought Elena. She pushed the smaller girl back.

"Bonnie! What did you do to your hair?"

"Do you like it? I think it makes me look

taller." Bonnie fluffed up the already fluffy bangs and smiled, her brown eyes sparkling with excitement, her little heart-shaped face alight.

Elena moved on. "Meredith. You haven't changed at all."

This hug was equally warm on both sides. She had missed Meredith more than anyone, Elena thought, looking at the tall girl. Meredith never wore any makeup; but then, with perfect olive skin and heavy black lashes, she didn't need any. Right now she had one elegant eyebrow raised as she studied Elena.

"Well, your hair is two shades lighter from the sun. . . . But where's your tan? I thought you were living it up on the French Riviera."

"You know I never tan." Elena held up her hands for her own inspection. The skin was flawless, like porcelain, but almost as fair and translucent as Bonnie's.

"Just a minute; that reminds me," Bonnie interjected, snatching one of Elena's hands. "Guess what I learned from my cousin this summer?" Before anyone could speak, she informed them triumphantly: "Palm reading!"

There were groans, and some laughter.

"Laugh while you can," said Bonnie, not at all disturbed. "My cousin told me I'm psychic.

Now, let me see . . ." She peered into Elena's palm.

"Hurry up or we're going to be late," said Elena a bit impatiently.

"All right, all right. Now, this is your life line —or is it your heart line?" In the crowd, someone snickered. "Quiet; I'm reaching into the void. I see . . . I see . . ." All at once, Bonnie's face went blank, as if she were startled. Her brown eyes widened, but she no longer seemed to be staring at Elena's hand. It was as if she were looking *through* it—at something frightening.

"You will meet a tall, dark stranger," Meredith murmured from behind her. There was a flurry of giggles.

"Dark, yes, and a stranger . . . but not tall." Bonnie's voice was hushed and faraway.

"Although," she continued after a moment, looking puzzled, "he *was* tall, once." Her wide brown eyes lifted to Elena's in bewilderment. "But that's impossible . . . isn't it?" She dropped Elena's hand, almost flinging it away. "I don't want to see any more."

"Okay, show's over. Let's go," Elena told the others, vaguely irritated. She'd always felt psychic tricks were just that—tricks. So why was

14

she annoyed? Just because that morning she'd almost freaked out herself. . . .

The girls started toward the school building, but the roar of a finely tuned motor stopped them all in their tracks.

"Well, now," Caroline said, staring. "Quite a car."

"Quite a Porsche," Meredith corrected dryly.

The sleek black 911 Turbo purred through the parking lot, searching for a space, moving as lazily as a panther stalking prey.

When the car came to a stop, the door opened, and they glimpsed the driver.

"Oh, my God," Caroline whispered.

"You can say that again," breathed Bonnie.

From where she stood, Elena could see he had a lean, flat-muscled body. Faded jeans he probably had to peel off at night, tight T-shirt, and a leather jacket of unusual cut. His hair was wavy —and dark.

He wasn't tall, though. Just average height.

Elena let out her breath.

"Who *is* that masked man?" said Meredith. And the remark was apt—dark sunglasses completely covered the boy's eyes, shielding his face like a mask.

"That masked *stranger*," someone else said, and a babble of voices rose up.

"Do you see that jacket? That's Italian, as in Roma."

"How would you know? You've never been farther than Rome, New York, in your life!"

"Uh-oh. Elena's got that look again. The hunting look."

"Short-Dark-and-Handsome had better be careful."

"He isn't short; he's perfect!"

Through the chatter, Caroline's voice suddenly rang out. "Oh, come on, Elena. You've already got Matt. What more do you want? What can you do with two that you can't do with one?"

"The same thing—only longer," drawled Meredith, and the group dissolved into laughter.

The boy had locked his car and was walking toward school. Casually, Elena started after him, the other girls right behind her in a close-knit pack. For an instant, annoyance bubbled up inside her. Couldn't she go *anywhere* without a parade on her heels? But Meredith caught her eye, and she smiled in spite of herself.

"*Noblesse oblige*," Meredith said softly.

"What?"

"If you're going to be queen of the school, you have to put up with the consequences."

Elena frowned at this as they entered the building. A long corridor stretched before them, and a figure in jeans and leather jacket was disappearing through the office doorway up ahead. Elena slowed her pace as she walked up to the office, finally stopping to glance thoughtfully at the messages on the cork bulletin board by the door. There was a large window here, through which the entire office was visible.

The other girls were openly gazing through the window, and giggling. "Nice rear view." "That is *definitely* an Armani jacket." "You think he's from out of state?"

Elena was straining her ears for the boy's name. There seemed to be some kind of trouble in there: Mrs. Clarke, the admissions secretary, was looking at a list and shaking her head. The boy said something, and Mrs. Clarke lifted her hands in a "What can I say?" gesture. She ran a finger down the list and shook her head again, conclusively. The boy started to turn away, then turned back. And when Mrs. Clarke looked up at him, her expression changed.

The boy's sunglasses were now in his hand. Mrs. Clarke seemed startled by something; Elena could see her blink several times. Her lips opened and closed as if she were trying to speak.

Elena wished she could see more than the

back of the boy's head. Mrs. Clarke was fumbling through piles of paper now, looking dazed. At last she found a form of some kind and wrote on it, then turned it around and pushed it toward the boy.

The boy wrote briefly on the form—signing it, probably—and returned it. Mrs. Clarke stared at it a second, then fumbled through a new pile of papers, finally handing what looked like a class schedule to him. Her eyes never left the boy as he took it, inclined his head in thanks, and turned to the door.

Elena was wild with curiosity by now. What had just happened in there? And what did this stranger's face look like? But as he emerged from the office, he was settling his sunglasses in place again. Disappointment coursed through her.

Still, she could see the rest of his face as he paused in the doorway. The dark curly hair framed features so fine that they might have been taken from an old Roman coin or medallion. High cheekbones, classical straight nose . . . and a mouth to keep you awake at night, Elena thought. The upper lip was beautifully sculpted, a little sensitive, a whole lot sensual. The chatter of the girls in the hallway had stopped as if someone had thrown a switch.

Most of them were turning away from the boy

now, looking anywhere but at him. Elena held her place by the window and gave a little toss to her head, pulling the ribbon out of her hair so that it fell loose around her shoulders.

Without looking to either side, the boy moved on down the hallway. A chorus of sighs and whispers flared up the moment he was out of earshot.

Elena didn't hear any of it.

He'd walked right by her, she thought, dazed. Right by without a glance.

Dimly, she realized the bell was ringing. Meredith was tugging her arm.

"What?"

"I said here's your schedule. We've got trig on the second floor right now. Come on!"

Elena allowed Meredith to propel her down the corridor, up a flight of stairs, and into a classroom. She slid into an empty seat automatically and fixed her eyes on the teacher at the front without really seeing her. The shock still hadn't worn off.

He'd walked right by. Without a glance. She couldn't remember how long it had been since a boy had done that. They all looked, at least. Some whistled. Some stopped to talk. Some just stared.

And that had always been fine with Elena.

After all, what was more important than boys? They were the mark of how popular you were, of how beautiful you were. And they could be useful for all sorts of things. Sometimes they were exciting, but usually that didn't last long. Sometimes they were creeps from the beginning.

Most boys, Elena reflected, were like puppies. Adorable in their place, but expendable. A very few could be more than that, could become real friends. Like Matt.

Oh, Matt. Last year she'd hoped that he was the one she was looking for, the boy who could make her feel . . . well, something more. More than the rush of triumph at making a conquest, the pride in showing your new acquisition off to the other girls. And she *had* come to feel a strong affection for Matt. But over the summer, when she'd had time to think, she'd realized it was the affection of a cousin or sister.

Ms. Halpern was passing out trigonometry books. Elena took hers mechanically and wrote her name inside, still wrapped in thought.

She liked Matt more than any other boy she'd known. And that was why she was going to have to tell him it was over.

She hadn't known how to tell him in a letter. She didn't know how to tell him now. It wasn't that she was afraid he'd kick up a fuss; he just wouldn't understand. She didn't really understand herself.

It was as if she were always reaching for . . . something. Only, when she thought she'd got it, it wasn't there. Not with Matt, not with any of the boys she'd had.

And then she had to start all over again. Fortunately, there was always fresh material. No boy had ever resisted her successfully, and no boy had ever ignored her. Until now.

Until now. Remembering that moment in the hall, Elena found that her fingers were clenched on the pen she held. She still couldn't believe he'd brushed by her that way.

The bell rang and everyone flooded out of the classroom, but Elena paused in the doorway. She bit her lip, scanning the river of students flowing through the hall. Then she spotted one of the hangers-on from the parking lot.

"Frances! Come here."

Frances came eagerly, her plain face brightening.

"Listen, Frances, you remember that boy this morning?"

"With the Porsche and the—er—assets? How could I forget?"

"Well, I want his class schedule. Get it from

the office if you can, or copy it from him if you have to. But do it!"

Frances looked surprised for a moment, then grinned and nodded. "Okay, Elena. I'll try. I'll meet you at lunch if I can get it."

"Thanks." Elena watched the girl go.

"You know, you really are crazy," Meredith's voice said in her ear.

"What's the use of being queen of the school if you can't pull a little rank sometimes?" returned Elena calmly. "Where do I go now?"

"General Business. Here, take it yourself." Meredith thrust a schedule at her. "I've got to run for chemistry. Later!"

General Business and the rest of the morning passed in a blur. Elena had hoped to catch another glimpse of the new student, but he was in none of her classes. Matt *was* in one, and she felt a pang as his blue eyes met hers with a smile.

At the lunch bell, she nodded greetings right and left as she walked to the cafeteria. Caroline was outside, posed casually against a wall with chin up, shoulders back, hips forward. The two boys she was talking to fell silent and nudged each other as Elena approached.

"Hi," Elena said briefly to the boys; and to Caroline: "Ready to go in and eat?"

Caroline's green eyes barely flickered toward

Elena, and she pushed glossy auburn hair out of her face. "What, at the *royal table?*" she said.

Elena was taken aback. She and Caroline had been friends since kindergarten, and they had always competed with each other good-naturedly. But lately something had happened to Caroline. She'd begun to take the rivalry more and more seriously. And now Elena was surprised at the bitterness in the other girl's voice.

"Well, it's hardly as if you were a commoner," she said lightly.

"Oh, you're so right about that," said Caroline, turning to face Elena fully. Those green cat-eyes were slitted and smoky, and Elena was shocked by the hostility she saw there. The two boys smiled uneasily and edged away.

Caroline didn't seem to notice. "A lot of things changed while you were gone this summer, Elena," she continued. "And just maybe your time on the throne is running out."

Elena had flushed; she could feel it. She struggled to keep her voice steady. "Maybe," she said. "But I wouldn't buy a scepter just yet if I were you, Caroline." She turned and went into the lunchroom.

It was a relief to see Meredith and Bonnie, and Frances beside them. Elena felt her cheeks cool as she selected her lunch and went to join them. She wouldn't let Caroline upset her; she wouldn't think of Caroline at all.

"I got it," said Frances, waving a piece of paper as Elena sat down.

"And I have some good stuff," said Bonnie importantly. "Elena, listen to this. He's in my biology class, and I sit right across from him. And his name is Stefan, Stefan Salvatore, and he's from Italy, and he's boarding with old Mrs. Flowers on the edge of town." She sighed. "He is *so* romantic. Caroline dropped her books, and he picked them up for her."

Elena made a wry face. "How clumsy of Caroline. What else happened?"

"Well, that's all. He didn't really talk to her. He's ver-r-ry mysterious, you see. Mrs. Endicott, my biology teacher, tried to get him to take off his glasses, but he wouldn't. He has a medical condition."

"What kind of medical condition?"

"*I* don't know. Maybe it's terminal and his days are numbered. Wouldn't that be romantic?"

"Oh, very," said Meredith.

Elena was looking over Frances's sheet of paper, biting her lip. "He's in my seventh period, History of Europe. Anybody else have that class?"

"I do," said Bonnie. "And I think Caroline does, too. Oh, and maybe Matt; he said something yesterday about how it was just his luck, getting Mr. Tanner."

Marvelous, Elena thought, picking up a fork and stabbing at her mashed potatoes. It looked as if seventh period was going to be *extremely* interesting.

Stefan was glad the school day was almost over. He wanted to get out of these crowded rooms and corridors, just for a few minutes.

So many minds. The pressure of so many thought patterns, so many mental voices surrounding him, was making him dizzy. It had been years since he had been in a swarm of people like this.

One mind in particular stood out from the others. She had been among those watching him in the main corridor of the school building. He didn't know what she looked like, but her personality was powerful. He felt sure he'd recognize it again.

So far, at least, he'd survived the first day of the masquerade. He'd used the Powers only twice, and then sparingly. But he was tired, and, he admitted ruefully, hungry. The rabbit hadn't been enough.

Worry about that later. He found his last classroom and sat down. And immediately he felt the presence of that mind again.

It glowed at the edge of his consciousness, a golden light, soft and yet vibrant. And, for the first time, he could locate the girl it was coming from. She was seated right in front of him.

Even as he thought it, she turned around and he saw her face. It was all he could do not to gasp in shock.

Katherine! But of course it couldn't be. Katherine was dead; no one knew that better than he did.

Still, the resemblance was uncanny. That pale golden hair, so fair it almost seemed to shimmer. That creamy skin, which had always made him think of swans, or alabaster, flushing faintly pink over the cheekbones. And the eyes . . . Katherine's eyes had been a color he had never seen before; darker than sky blue, as rich as the lapis lazuli in her jeweled headband. This girl had those same eyes.

And they were fixed directly on his as she smiled.

He looked down from the smile quickly. Of all things, he did not want to think about Katherine. He didn't want to look at this girl who reminded him of her, and he didn't want to feel her presence any longer. He kept his eyes on the desk, blocking his mind as strongly as he knew how. And at last, slowly, she turned around again.

She was hurt. Even through the blocks, he could feel that. He didn't care. In fact, he was glad of it, and he hoped it would keep her away from him. Other than that, he had no feelings about her at all.

He kept telling himself this as he sat, the droning voice of the teacher pouring over him unheard. But he could smell a subtle hint of some perfume—violets, he thought. And her slender white neck was bowed over her book, the fair hair falling on either side of it.

In anger and frustration he recognized the seductive feeling in his teeth—more a tickling or a tingling than an ache. It was hunger, a specific hunger. And not one he was about to indulge.

The teacher was pacing about the room like a ferret, asking questions, and Stefan deliberately fixed his attention on the man. At first he was puzzled, for although none of the students knew the answers, the questions kept coming. Then he realized that that was the man's purpose. To shame the students with what they didn't know.

Just now he'd found another victim, a small

girl with clusters of red curls and a heart-shaped face. Stefan watched in distaste as the teacher badgered her with questions. She looked wretched as he turned away from her to address the entire class.

"You see what I mean? You think you're pretty hot stuff; you're seniors now, ready to graduate. Well, let me tell you, some of you aren't ready to graduate kindergarten. Like this!" He gestured toward the red-haired girl. "No idea about the French Revolution. Thinks Marie Antoinette was a silent film star."

Students all around Stefan were shifting uncomfortably. He could feel the resentment in their minds, and the humiliation. And the fear. They were all afraid of this thin little man with eyes like a weasel, even the husky boys who were taller than he was.

"All right, let's try another era." The teacher swung back to the same girl he'd been questioning. "During the Renaissance—" He broke off. "You *do* know what the Renaissance is, don't you? The period between the thirteenth and seventeenth centuries, in which Europe rediscovered the great ideas of ancient Greece and Rome? The period that produced so many of Europe's greatest artists and thinkers?" When the girl nodded confusedly, he continued. "During the Renaissance, what would students your age be doing at school? Well? Any idea at all? Any guesses?"

The girl swallowed hard. With a weak smile she said, "Playing football?"

At the ensuing laughter, the teacher's face darkened. "Hardly!" he snapped, and the classroom quieted. "You think this is a joke? Well, in those days, students your age would already be proficient in several languages. They would also have mastered logic, mathematics, astronomy, philosophy, and grammar. They would be ready to go on to a university, in which every course was taught in Latin. Football would be absolutely the last thing on—"

"Excuse me."

The quiet voice stopped the teacher in midharangue. Everyone turned to stare at Stefan.

"What? What did you say?"

"I said, excuse me," Stefan repeated, removing his glasses and standing up. "But you're wrong. Students in the Renaissance were encouraged to participate in games. They were taught that a healthy body goes with a healthy mind. And they certainly played team sports, like cricket, tennis—and even football." He turned to the red-haired girl and smiled, and she smiled back gratefully. To the teacher, he added, "But the most important things they learned were good manners and courtesy. I'm sure your book will tell you that."

Students were grinning. The teacher's face was red with blood, and he was sputtering. But Stefan continued to hold his eyes, and after another minute it was the teacher who looked away.

The bell rang.

Stefan put his glasses on quickly and gathered his books. He'd already drawn more attention to himself than he should, and he didn't want to have to look at the blond girl again. Besides, he needed to get out of here quickly; there was a familiar burning sensation in his veins.

As he reached the door, someone shouted, "Hey! Did they really play football back then?"

He couldn't help throwing a grin over his shoulder. "Oh, yes. Sometimes with the severed heads of prisoners of war."

Elena watched him as he went. He'd deliberately turned away from her. He'd snubbed her on purpose, and in front of Caroline, who'd been watching like a hawk. Tears burned in her eyes, but at that moment only one thought burned in her mind.

She'd have him, even if it killed her. If it killed both of them, she'd have him.

Three

The first light of dawn was streaking the night sky with pink and palest green. Stefan watched it from the window of his room in the boarding house. He had rented this room specifically because of the trapdoor in the ceiling, a trapdoor that opened onto the widow's walk on the roof above. Just now that door was open, and a cool damp wind blew down the ladder below it. Stefan was fully dressed, but not because he was up early. He had never been to sleep.

He'd just returned from the woods, and a few scraps of wet leaf clung to the side of his boot. He brushed them off fastidiously. The comments of the students yesterday had not escaped him, and he knew they had been staring at his clothes. He had always dressed in the best, not merely out of vanity, but because it was the right thing to do. His tutor had often said it: *An aristocrat should dress as befits his position. If he does not, he is showing contempt for others.* Everyone had a place in the world, and his place had once been among the nobility. Once.

Why was he dwelling on these things? Of course, he should have realized that playing the role of a student was likely to bring his own student days back. Now the memories came thick and fast, as if he were skimming through the pages of a journal, his eyes catching an entry here and there. One flashed before him vividly now: his father's face when Damon had announced he was quitting the University. He would never forget that. He had never seen his father so angry. . . .

"What do you mean, you are not going back?" Giuseppe was usually a fair man, but he had a temper, and his elder son brought out the violence in him.

Just now that son was dabbing at his lips with a saffron-colored silk handkerchief. "I would have thought even you could understand such a simple sentence, father. Shall I repeat it in Latin for you?"

"Damon—" Stefan began tightly, appalled at this disrespect. But his father interrupted.

"You are telling me that I, Giuseppe, Conte di Salvatore, will have to face my friends knowing that my son is a *scioparto*? A ne'er-do-well? An idler who makes no useful contribution to Florence?" Servants were edging away as Giuseppe worked himself into a rage.

Damon did not even blink. "Apparently. If you can call those who fawn on you in the hopes that you will lend them money your friends."

"Sporco parassito!" cried Giuseppe, rising from his chair. "Is it not bad enough that when you *are* at school you waste your time and my money? Oh, yes, I know all about the gambling, the jousting, the women. And I know that if it were not for your secretary and your tutors you would be failing every course. But now you mean to disgrace me utterly. And why? Why?" His large hand whipped up to grasp Damon's chin. "So that you may return to your hunting and hawking?"

Stefan had to give his brother credit; Damon did not wince. He stood, almost lounging in his father's grip, every inch the aristocrat, from the elegantly plain cap on his dark head to his ermine-trimmed cloak to his soft leather shoes. His upper lip was curved in a line of pure arrogance.

You've gone too far this time, thought Stefan,

watching the two men whose eyes were locked together. Even you won't be able to charm your way out this time.

But just then there was a light step in the study doorway. Turning, Stefan had been dazzled by eyes the color of lapis lazuli, framed with long golden lashes. It was Katherine. Her father, Baron von Swartzschild, had brought her from the cold lands of the German princes to the Italian countryside, hoping it would help her recover from a prolonged illness. And since the day she had arrived, everything had changed for Stefan.

"I beg your pardon. I did not mean to intrude." Her voice was soft and clear. She made a slight motion as if to leave.

"No, don't go. Stay," Stefan said quickly. He wanted to say more, to catch her hand—but he didn't dare. Not with his father here. All he could do was gaze into those jewellike blue eyes that were raised to his.

"Yes, stay," Giuseppe said, and Stefan saw that his father's thunderous expression had lightened and that he had released Damon. He stepped forward, straightening the heavy folds of his long fur-trimmed gown. "Your father should be returning from his business in the city today, and he will be delighted to see you. But your cheeks are pale, little Katherine. You are not ill again, I hope?"

"You know I am always pale, sir. I do not use rouge like your bold Italian girls."

"You don't need it," said Stefan before he could stop himself, and Katherine smiled at him. She was so beautiful. An ache began in his chest.

His father continued, "And I see all too little of you during the day. You seldom give us the pleasure of your company until twilight."

"I have my studies and devotions in my own rooms, sir," said Katherine quietly, her lashes dropping. Stefan knew this was not true, but he said nothing; he would never betray Katherine's secret. She looked up at his father again. "But I am here now, sir."

"Yes, yes, that is true. And I must see that tonight we have a very special meal for your father's return. Damon . . . we will speak later." As Giuseppe motioned to a servant and strode out, Stefan turned to Katherine in delight. It was seldom they could speak to each other without the presence of his father or of Gudren, her stolid German maid.

But what Stefan saw then was like a blow to his stomach. Katherine was smiling—the little secret smile that she had often shared with him.

36

But she was not looking at him. She was looking at Damon.

Stefan hated his brother at that moment, hated Damon's dark beauty and grace and the sensuality that drew women to him like moths to a flame. He wanted, in that instant, to strike Damon, to smash that beauty to pieces. Instead he had to stand and watch as Katherine moved slowly toward his brother, step by step, her golden brocade gown whispering on the tiled floor.

And even as he watched, Damon held out a hand to Katherine, and smiled the cruel smile of triumph. . . .

Stefan turned away from the window sharply. Why was he reopening old wounds? But, even as he thought it, he drew out the slender gold chain he wore under his shirt. His thumb and forefinger caressed the ring that hung from it, then he held it up to the light.

The little circlet was exquisitely worked in gold, and five centuries had not dimmed its luster. It was set with one stone, a lapis the size of his little fingernail. Stefan looked at it, then at the heavy silver ring, also set with lapis, on his own hand. In his chest was a familiar tightness.

He could not forget the past, and he didn't really wish to. Despite everything that had happened, he cherished Katherine's memory. But there was one memory he must truly not disturb, one page of the journal he must not turn. If he had to relive that horror, that . . . abomination, he would go mad. As he had been mad that day, that final day, when he had looked upon his own damnation . . .

Stefan leaned against the window, his forehead pressed to its coolness. His tutor had had another saying: *Evil will never find peace. It may triumph, but it will never find peace.*

Why had he even come to Fell's Church?

He had hoped to find peace here, but that was impossible. He would never be accepted, he would never rest. Because he was evil. He could not change what he was.

Elena was up even earlier than usual that morning. She could hear Aunt Judith pottering about in her room, getting ready for her shower. Margaret was still fast asleep, curled up like a little mouse in her bed. Elena passed her younger sister's half-open door noiselessly and continued down the hallway to let herself out of the house.

The air was fresh and clear this morning; the

quince tree was inhabited only by the usual jays and sparrows. Elena, who had gone to bed with a throbbing headache, lifted her face to the clean blue sky and breathed deeply.

She felt much better than she had yesterday. She'd promised to meet Matt before school, and though she wasn't looking forward to it she was sure it was going to be all right.

Matt lived only two streets away from the high school. It was a simple frame house, like all the others on that street, except that maybe the swing on the porch was a little shabbier, the paint a little more peeled. Matt was already standing outside, and for a moment her heart picked up at the sight of him as it used to.

He *was* good-looking. There was no doubt about that. Not in the stunning, almost disturbing way that—that some people were, but in a healthy American way. Matt Honeycutt was all-American. His blond hair was cropped short for the football season, and his skin was sunburnt from working outdoors on his grandparents' farm. His blue eyes were honest and straightforward. And just today, as he held out his arms to hug her gently, they were a little sad.

"You want to come inside?"

"No. Let's just walk," Elena said. They went side by side without touching. Maples and black walnut trees lined this street, and the air still had a morning hush. Elena watched her feet on the wet sidewalk, feeling suddenly uncertain. She didn't know how to start after all.

"So you still haven't told me about France," he said.

"Oh, it was great," said Elena. She glanced sideways at him. He was looking at the sidewalk, too. "Everything about it was great," she continued, trying to put some enthusiasm in her voice. "The people, the food, everything. It was really . . ." Her voice trailed off, and she laughed nervously.

"Yeah, I know. Great," he finished for her. He stopped and stood looking down at his scuffed tennis shoes. Elena recognized them from last year. Matt's family barely got by; maybe he hadn't been able to afford new shoes. She looked up to find those steady blue eyes on her face.

"You know, *you* look pretty great right now," he said.

Elena opened her mouth in dismay, but he was speaking again.

"And I guess you have something to tell me." She stared at him, and he smiled, a crooked, rueful smile. Then he held out his arms again.

"Oh, *Matt*," she said, hugging him hard. She

stepped back to look into his face. "Matt, you are the nicest guy I've ever met. I don't deserve you."

"Oh, so that's why you're dumping me," said Matt as they started walking again. "Because I'm too good for you. I should have realized that before."

She punched him in the arm. "No, that isn't why, and I am not dumping you. We're going to be friends, right?"

"Oh, sure. Oh, absolutely."

"Because that's what I've realized we are." She stopped, looking up at him again. "Good friends. Be honest, now, Matt, isn't that how you really feel about me?"

He looked at her, then rolled his eyes heavenward. "Can I take the Fifth on that?" he said. As Elena's face fell, he added, "It doesn't have anything to do with that new guy, does it?"

"No," Elena said after a hesitation, and then added quickly, "I haven't even met him yet. I don't know him."

"But you want to. No, don't say it." He put an arm around her and gently turned her. "Come on, let's head toward school. If we have time, I'll even buy you a doughnut."

As they walked, something thrashed in the walnut tree above them. Matt whistled and pointed. "Look at that! Biggest crow I've ever seen."

Elena looked, but it was already gone.

School that day was merely a convenient place for Elena to review her plan.

She had woken up this morning knowing what to do. And today she gathered as much information as she could on the subject of Stefan Salvatore. Which wasn't hard, because everyone at Robert E. Lee was talking about him.

It was common knowledge that he'd had some sort of run-in with the admissions secretary yesterday. And today he'd been called to the principal's office. Something about his papers. But the principal had sent him back to class (after, it was rumored, a long-distance call to Rome—or was it Washington?), and everything seemed to be settled now. Officially, at least.

When Elena arrived for Euro History class that afternoon, she was greeted by a low whistle in the hall. Dick Carter and Tyler Smallwood were loitering there. A couple of prize jerks, she thought, ignoring the whistle and their staring. They thought being tackle and safety on the varsity football team made them hot stuff. She kept an eye on them as she loitered in the corridor herself, refreshing her lipstick and fiddling with her compact. She'd given Bonnie her special instructions, and the plan was ready to be put into effect as soon as Stefan showed up. The compact mirror gave her a wonderful view of the hall behind her.

Still, she missed him coming somehow. He was beside her suddenly, and she snapped the compact shut as he passed. She meant to stop him, but something happened before she could. Stefan tensed—or, at least, there was something about him that seemed wary all at once. Just then Dick and Tyler stepped in front of the door to the history classroom. Blocking the way.

World-class jerks, thought Elena. Fuming, she glared at them over Stefan's shoulder.

They were enjoying the game, slouching in the doorway, pretending they were completely blind to Stefan standing there.

"Excuse me." It was the same tone he'd used with the history teacher. Quiet, detached.

Dick and Tyler looked at each other, then all around, as if hearing spirit voices.

"Scoozi?" Tyler said in a falsetto. "Scoozi me? Me scoozi? Jacuzzi?" They both laughed.

Elena watched muscles tighten under the T-shirt in front of her. This was completely unfair; they were both taller than Stefan, and Tyler was about twice as broad.

"Is there a problem here?" Elena was as startled as the boys were at the new voice behind her. She turned to see Matt. His blue eyes were hard.

Elena bit her lips on a smile as Tyler and Dick moved slowly, resentfully out of the way. Good old Matt, she thought. But now good old Matt was walking into class beside Stefan, and she was left following them, staring at the backs of *two* T-shirts. When they sat down, she slid into the desk behind Stefan, where she could watch him without being watched herself. Her plan would have to wait until after class.

Matt was rattling change in his pocket, which meant he wanted to say something.

"Uh, hey," he began at last, uncomfortably. "Those guys, you know . . ."

Stefan laughed. It was a bitter sound. "Who am I to judge?" There was more emotion in his voice than Elena had heard before, even when he had spoken to Mr. Tanner. And that emotion was raw unhappiness. "Anyway, why should I be welcome here?" he finished, almost to himself.

"Why shouldn't you be?" Matt had been staring at Stefan; now his jaw squared with decision.

"Listen," he said. "You were talking about football yesterday. Well, our star wide receiver tore a ligament yesterday afternoon, and we need a replacement. Tryouts are this afternoon. What do you think?"

"Me?" Stefan sounded caught off guard. "Ah . . . I don't know if I could."

"Can you run?"

"Can—?" Stefan half turned toward Matt, and Elena could see a faint hint of a smile curve his lips. "Yes."

"Can you catch?"

"Yes."

"That's all a wide receiver has to do. I'm the quarterback. If you can catch what I throw and run with it, you can play."

"I see." Stefan was actually almost smiling, and though Matt's mouth was serious his blue eyes were dancing. Astonished at herself, Elena realized she was jealous. There was a warmth between the two boys that shut her out completely.

But the next instant Stefan's smile disappeared. He said distantly, "Thank you . . . but no. I have other commitments."

At that moment, Bonnie and Caroline arrived and class started.

Throughout Tanner's lecture on Europe,

Elena repeated to herself, "Hello. I'm Elena Gilbert. I'm on the Senior Welcoming Committee, and I've been assigned to show you around the school. Now, you wouldn't want to get me in trouble, would you, by not letting me do my job?" That last with wide, wistful eyes—but only if he looked like he might try to get out of it. It was virtually foolproof. He was a sucker for maidens who needed to be rescued.

Halfway through class, the girl sitting to her right passed her a note. Elena opened it and recognized Bonnie's round, childish handwriting. It read: "I kept C. away for as long as I could. What happened? Did it work???"

Elena looked up to see Bonnie twisted around in her front-row seat. Elena pointed to the note and shook her head, mouthing, "After class."

It seemed a century until Tanner gave some last-minute instructions about oral reports and dismissed them. Then everybody sprang up at once. Here goes, thought Elena, and, with her heart pounding, she stepped squarely into Stefan's path, blocking the aisle so that he couldn't get around her.

Just like Dick and Tyler, she thought, feeling a hysterical urge to giggle. She looked up and found her eyes exactly on a level with his mouth.

Her mind went blank. What was it she was supposed to say? She opened her mouth, and somehow the words she'd been practicing came tumbling out. "Hi, I'm Elena Gilbert, and I'm on the Senior Welcoming Committee and I've been assigned—"

"I'm sorry; I don't have time." For a minute, she couldn't believe he was speaking, that he wasn't even going to give her a chance to finish. Her mouth went right on with the speech.

"—to show you around the school—"

"I'm sorry; I can't. I have to—to get to football tryouts." Stefan turned to Matt, who was standing by looking amazed. "You said they were right after school, didn't you?"

"Yes," Matt said slowly. "But—"

"Then I'd better get moving. Maybe you could show me the way."

Matt looked helplessly at Elena, then shrugged. "Well . . . sure. Come on." He glanced back once as they left. Stefan didn't.

Elena found herself looking around at a circle of interested observers, including Caroline, who was openly smirking. Elena felt a numbness in her body and a fullness in her throat. She couldn't stand to be here for one more second. She turned and walked as quickly as she could from the room.

Four

By the time Elena reached her locker, the numbness was wearing off and the lump in her throat was trying to dissolve into tears. But she wouldn't cry at school, she told herself, she *wouldn't*. After closing her locker, she made for the main exit.

For the second day in a row, she was coming home from school right after the last bell, and alone. Aunt Judith wouldn't be able to cope. But when Elena reached her house, Aunt Judith's car was not in the driveway; she and Margaret must have gone out to the market. The house was still and peaceful as Elena let herself in.

She was glad for that stillness; she wanted to be alone right now. But, on the other hand, she didn't exactly know what to do with herself.

Now that she finally *could* cry, she found that tears wouldn't come. She let her backpack sag to the floor in the front hall and walked slowly into the living room.

It was a handsome, impressive room, the only part of the house besides Elena's bedroom that belonged to the original structure. That first house had been built before 1861, and had been almost completely burned in the Civil War. All that could be saved was this room, with its elaborate fireplace framed by scrolled molding, and the big bedroom above. Elena's father's great-grandfather had built a new house, and Gilberts had lived in it ever since.

Elena turned to look out of one of the ceiling-to-floor windows. The glass was so old that it was thick and wavery, and everything outside was distorted, looking slightly tipsy. She remembered the first time her father had showed her that wavery old glass, when she had been younger than Margaret was now.

The fullness in her throat was back, but still no tears would come. Everything inside her was contradictory. She didn't want company, and yet she was achingly lonely. She *did* want to think, but now that she was trying to, her thoughts eluded her like mice running from a white owl.

White owl . . . hunting bird . . . flesh eater . . . crow, she thought. "Biggest crow I've ever seen," Matt had said.

Her eyes stung again. Poor Matt. She'd hurt him, but he'd been so nice about it. He'd even been nice to Stefan.

Stefan. Her heart thudded once, hard, squeezing two hot tears out of her eyes. There, she was crying at last. She was crying with anger and humiliation and frustration—and what else?

What had she really lost today? What did she really feel for this stranger, this Stefan Salvatore? He was a challenge, yes, and that made him different, interesting. Stefan was exotic . . . exciting.

Funny, that was what guys had sometimes told Elena *she* was. And later she heard from them, or from their friends or sisters, how nervous they were before going out with her, how their palms got sweaty and their stomachs were full of butterflies. Elena had always found such stories amusing. No boy she'd ever met in her life had made her nervous.

But when she'd spoken to Stefan today, her pulse had been racing, her knees weak. Her palms had been wet. And there hadn't been butterflies in her stomach—there had been bats.

She was interested in the guy because he

made her feel nervous? Not a very good reason, Elena, she told herself. In fact, a very bad reason.

But there was also that mouth. That sculpted mouth that made her knees weak with something entirely different than nervousness. And that night-dark hair—her fingers itched to weave themselves into its softness. That lithe, flat-muscled body, those long legs . . . and that *voice*. It was his voice that had decided her yesterday, making her absolutely determined to have him. His voice had been cool and disdainful when talking to Mr. Tanner, but strangely compelling for all that. She wondered if it could turn night-dark as well, and how it would sound saying her name, whispering her name. . . .

"Elena!"

Elena jumped, her reverie shattered. But it wasn't Stefan Salvatore calling her, it was Aunt Judith rattling the front door open.

"Elena? Elena!" And that was Margaret, her voice shrill and piping. "Are you home?"

Misery welled up in Elena again, and she glanced around the kitchen. She couldn't face her aunt's worried questions or Margaret's innocent cheerfulness right now. Not with her eyelashes wet and new tears threatening any minute. She made a lightning decision and quietly slipped out the back door as the front door banged shut.

Once off the back porch and into the yard, she hesitated. She didn't want to run into anyone she knew. But where could she go to be alone?

The answer came almost instantly. Of course. She'd go see Mom and Dad.

It was a fairly long walk, almost to the edge of town, but over the last three years it had become familiar to Elena. She crossed over Wickery Bridge and climbed up the hill, past the ruined church, then down into the little valley below.

This part of the cemetery was well-kept; it was the old section that was allowed to run slightly wild. Here, the grass was neatly trimmed, and bouquets of flowers made splashes of bright color. Elena sat down by the big marble headstone with "Gilbert" carved into the front.

"Hi, Mom. Hi, Dad," she whispered. She leaned over to place a purple impatiens blossom she'd picked along the way in front of the marker. Then she curled her legs under her and just sat.

She'd come here often after the accident. Margaret had been only one at the time of the car crash; she didn't really remember them. But

Elena did. Now she let her mind leaf back through memories, and the lump in her throat swelled, and the tears came easier. She missed them so much, still. Mother, so young and beautiful, and Father, with a smile that crinkled up his eyes.

She was lucky to have Aunt Judith, of course. It wasn't every aunt who would quit her job and move back into a little town to take care of two orphaned nieces. And Robert, Aunt Judith's fiancé, was more like a stepfather to Margaret than an uncle-to-be by marriage.

But Elena remembered her parents. Sometimes, right after the funeral, she had come out here to rage at them, angry with them for being so stupid as to get themselves killed. That was when she hadn't known Aunt Judith very well, and had felt there was nowhere on earth she belonged anymore.

Where did she belong now? she wondered. The easy answer was, here, in Fell's Church, where she'd lived all her life. But lately the easy answer seemed wrong. Lately she felt there must be something else out there for her, some place she would recognize at once and call home.

A shadow fell over her, and she looked up, startled. For an instant, the two figures standing over her were alien, unfamiliar, vaguely menacing. She stared, frozen.

"Elena," said the smaller figure fussily, hands on hips, "sometimes I *worry* about you, I really do."

Elena blinked and then laughed shortly. It was Bonnie and Meredith. "What does a person have to do to get a little privacy around here?" she said as they sat down.

"Tell us to go away," suggested Meredith, but Elena just shrugged. Meredith and Bonnie had often come out here to find her in the months after the accident. Suddenly, she felt glad about that, and grateful to them both. If nowhere else, she belonged with the friends who cared about her. She didn't mind if they knew she had been crying, and she accepted the crumpled tissue Bonnie offered her and wiped her eyes. The three of them sat together in silence for a little while, watching the wind ruffle the stand of oak trees at the edge of the cemetery.

"I'm sorry about what happened," Bonnie said at last, in a soft voice. "That was really terrible."

"And your middle name is 'Tact,'" said Meredith. "It couldn't have been that bad, Elena."

"You weren't there." Elena felt herself go hot all over again at the memory. "It *was* terrible.

But I don't care anymore," she added flatly, defiantly. "I'm finished with him. I don't want him anyway."

"Elena!"

"I don't, Bonnie. He obviously thinks he's too good for—for Americans. So he can just take those designer sunglasses and . . ."

There were snorts of laughter from the other girls. Elena wiped her nose and shook her head. "So," she said to Bonnie, determinedly changing the subject, "at least Tanner seemed in a better mood today."

Bonnie looked martyred. "Do you know that he made me sign up to be the very first one to give my oral report? I don't care, though; I'm going to do mine on the druids, and—"

"On the what?"

"*Droo*-ids. The weird old guys who built Stonehenge and did magic and stuff in ancient England. I'm descended from them, and that's why I'm psychic."

Meredith snorted, but Elena frowned at the blade of grass she was twirling between her fingers. "Bonnie, did you really see something yesterday in my palm?" she asked abruptly.

Bonnie hesitated. "I don't know," she said at last. "I—I *thought* I did then. But sometimes my imagination runs away with me."

"She knew you were here," said Meredith unexpectedly. "I thought of looking at the coffee shop, but Bonnie said, 'She's at the cemetery.'"

"Did I?" Bonnie looked faintly surprised but impressed. "Well, there you see. My grandmother in Edinburgh has the second sight and so do I. It always skips a generation."

"And you're descended from the druids," Meredith said solemnly.

"Well, it's true! In Scotland they keep up the old traditions. You wouldn't *believe* some of the things my grandmother does. She has a way to find out who you're going to marry and when you're going to die. She told me I'm going to die early."

"Bonnie!"

"She did. I'm going to be young and beautiful in my coffin. Don't you think that's romantic?"

"No, I don't. I think it's disgusting," said Elena. The shadows were getting longer, and the wind had a chill to it now.

"So who are you going to marry, Bonnie?" Meredith put in deftly.

"I don't know. My grandmother told me the ritual for finding out, but I never tried it. Of course"—Bonnie struck a sophisticated pose—"he has to be outrageously rich and totally gorgeous. Like our mysterious dark stranger, for example. Particularly if nobody else wants him." She cast a wicked glance at Elena.

Elena refused the bait. "What about Tyler Smallwood?" she murmured innocently. "His father's certainly rich enough."

"And he's not bad-looking," agreed Meredith solemnly. "That is, of course, if you're an animal lover. All those big white teeth."

The girls looked at each other and then simultaneously burst into laughter. Bonnie threw a handful of grass at Meredith, who brushed it off and threw a dandelion back at her. Somewhere in the middle of it, Elena realized that she was going to be all right. She was herself again, not lost, not a stranger, but Elena Gilbert, the queen of Robert E. Lee. She pulled the apricot ribbon out of her hair and shook the hair free about her face.

"I've decided what to do *my* oral report on," she said, watching with narrow eyes as Bonnie finger-combed grass out of her curls.

"What?" said Meredith.

Elena tilted her chin up to gaze at the red and purple sky above the hill. She took a thoughtful breath and let the suspense build for a moment. Then she said coolly, "The Italian Renaissance."

Bonnie and Meredith stared at her, then

looked at each other and burst into whoops of laughter again.

"Aha," said Meredith when they recovered. "So the tiger returneth."

Elena gave her a feral grin. Her shaken confidence had returned to her. And though she didn't understand it herself, she knew one thing: she wasn't going to let Stefan Salvatore get away alive.

"All right," she said briskly. "Now, listen, you two. Nobody else can know about this, or I'll be the laughingstock of the school. And Caroline would just love any excuse to make me look ridiculous. But I *do* still want him, and I'm going to have him. I don't know how yet, but I am. Until I come up with a plan, though, we're going to give him the cold shoulder."

"Oh, *we* are?"

"Yes, *we* are. You can't have him, Bonnie; he's mine. And I have to be able to trust you completely."

"Wait a minute," said Meredith, a glint in her eye. She unclasped the cloisonné pin from her blouse, then, holding up her thumb, made a quick jab. "Bonnie, give me your hand."

"Why?" said Bonnie, eyeing the pin suspiciously.

"Because I want to marry you. Why do you think, idiot?"

"But—but— Oh, all *right*. Ow!"

"Now you, Elena." Meredith pricked Elena's thumb efficiently, and then squeezed it to get a drop of blood. "Now," she continued, looking at the other two with sparkling dark eyes, "we all press our thumbs together and swear. Especially you, Bonnie. Swear to keep this secret and to do whatever Elena asks in relation to Stefan."

"Look, swearing with blood is dangerous," Bonnie protested seriously. "It means you have to stick to your oath no matter what happens, no matter *what*, Meredith."

"I know," said Meredith grimly. "That's why I'm telling you to do it. I remember what happened with Michael Martin."

Bonnie made a face. "That was years ago, and we broke up right away anyway and—Oh, all right. I'll swear." Closing her eyes, she said, "I swear to keep this a secret and to do anything Elena asks about Stefan."

Meredith repeated the oath. And Elena, staring at the pale shadows of their thumbs joined together in the gathering dusk, took a long breath and said softly, "And I swear not to rest until he belongs to me."

A gust of cold wind blew through the cemetery, fanning the girls' hair out and sending dry leaves fluttering on the ground. Bonnie gasped and pulled back, and they all looked around, then giggled nervously.

"It's dark," said Elena, surprised.

"We'd better get started home," Meredith said, refastening her pin as she stood up. Bonnie stood, too, putting the tip of her thumb into her mouth.

"Good-bye," said Elena softly, facing the headstone. The purple blossom was a blur on the ground. She picked up the apricot ribbon that lay next to it, turned, and nodded to Bonnie and Meredith. "Let's go."

Silently, they headed up the hill toward the ruined church. The oath sworn in blood had given them all a solemn feeling, and as they passed the ruined church Bonnie shivered. With the sun down, the temperature had dropped abruptly, and the wind was rising. Each gust sent whispers through the grass and made the ancient oak trees rattle their dangling leaves.

"I'm freezing," Elena said, pausing for a moment by the black hole that had once been the church door and looking down at the landscape below.

The moon had not yet risen, and she could just make out the old graveyard and Wickery

Bridge beyond it. The old graveyard dated from Civil War days, and many of the headstones bore the names of soldiers. It had a wild look to it; brambles and tall weeds grew on the graves, and ivy vines swarmed over crumbling granite. Elena had never liked it.

"It looks different, doesn't it? In the dark, I mean," she said unsteadily. She didn't know how to say what she really meant, that it was not a place for the living.

"We could go the long way," said Meredith. "But that would mean another twenty minutes of walking."

"I don't mind going this way," said Bonnie, swallowing hard. "I always said I wanted to be buried down there in the old one."

"Will you stop talking about being buried!" Elena snapped, and she started down the hill. But the farther down the narrow path she got, the more uncomfortable she felt. She slowed until Bonnie and Meredith caught up with her. As they neared the first headstone, her heart began beating fast. She tried to ignore it, but her whole skin was tingling with awareness and the fine hairs on her arms were standing up. Between the gusts of wind, every sound seemed horribly magnified; the crunching of their feet on the leaf-strewn path was deafening.

The ruined church was a black silhouette behind them now. The narrow path led between the lichen-encrusted headstones, many of which stood taller than Meredith. Big enough for something to hide behind, thought Elena uneasily. Some of the tombstones themselves were unnerving, like the one with the cherub that looked like a real baby, except that its head had fallen off and had been carefully placed by its body. The wide granite eyes of the head were blank. Elena couldn't look away from it, and her heart began to pound.

"Why are we stopping?" said Meredith.

"I just . . . I'm sorry," Elena murmured, but when she forced herself to turn she immediately stiffened. "Bonnie?" she said. "Bonnie, what's wrong?"

Bonnie was staring straight out into the graveyard, her lips parted, her eyes as wide and blank as the stone cherub's. Fear washed through Elena's stomach. "Bonnie, stop it. Stop it! It's not funny."

Bonnie made no reply.

"Bonnie!" said Meredith. She and Elena looked at each other, and suddenly Elena knew she had to get away. She whirled to start down the path, but a strange voice spoke behind her, and she jerked around.

"Elena," the voice said. It wasn't Bonnie's voice, but it came from Bonnie's mouth. Pale in the darkness, Bonnie was still staring out into the graveyard. There was no expression on her face at all.

"Elena," the voice said again, and added, as Bonnie's head turned toward her, "there's someone waiting out there for you."

Elena never quite knew what happened in the next few minutes. Something seemed to move out among the dark humped shapes of the headstones, shifting and rising between them. Elena screamed and Meredith cried out, and then they were both running, and Bonnie was running with them, screaming, too.

Elena pounded down the narrow path, stumbling on rocks and clumps of grass root. Bonnie was sobbing for breath behind her, and Meredith, calm and cynical Meredith, was panting wildly. There was a sudden thrashing and a shriek in an oak tree above them, and Elena found that she could run faster.

"There's something behind us," cried Bonnie shrilly. "Oh, God, what's happening?"

"Get to the bridge," gasped Elena through the fire in her lungs. She didn't know why, but she felt they had to make it there. "Don't stop,

Bonnie! Don't look behind you!" She grabbed the other girl's sleeve and pulled her around.

"I can't make it," Bonnie sobbed, clutching her side, her pace faltering.

"Yes, you can," snarled Elena, grabbing Bonnie's sleeve again and forcing her to keep moving. "Come on. *Come on!*"

She saw the silver gleam of water before them. And there was the clearing between the oak trees, and the bridge just beyond. Elena's legs were wobbling and her breath was whistling in her throat, but she wouldn't let herself lag behind. Now she could see the wooden planks of the footbridge. The bridge was twenty feet away from them, ten feet away, five.

"We made it," panted Meredith, feet thundering on the wood.

"Don't stop! Get to the other side!"

The bridge creaked as they ran staggering across it, their steps echoing across the water. When she jumped onto packed dirt on the far shore, Elena let go of Bonnie's sleeve at last, and allowed her legs to stumble to a halt.

Meredith was bent over, hands on thighs, deep-breathing. Bonnie was crying.

"What was it? Oh, what was it?" she said. "Is it still coming?"

"I thought you were the expert," Meredith

said unsteadily. "For God's sake, Elena, let's get out of here."

"No, it's all right now," Elena whispered. There were tears in her own eyes and she was shaking all over, but the hot breath at the back of her neck had gone. The river stretched between her and it, the waters a dark tumult. "It can't follow us here," she said.

Meredith stared at her, then at the other shore with its clustered oak trees, then at Bonnie. She wet her lips and laughed shortly. "Sure. It can't follow us. But let's go home anyway, all right? Unless you feel like spending the night out here."

Some unnameable feeling shuddered through Elena. "Not tonight, thanks," she said. She put an arm around Bonnie, who was still sniffling. "It's okay, Bonnie. We're safe now. Come on."

Meredith was looking across the river again. "You know, I don't see a thing back there," she said, her voice calmer. "Maybe there wasn't anything behind us at all; maybe we just panicked and scared ourselves. With a little help from the druid priestess here."

Elena said nothing as they started walking, keeping very close together on the dirt path. But she wondered. She wondered very much.

Five

The full moon was directly overhead when Stefan came back to the boarding house. He was giddy, almost reeling, both from fatigue and from the glut of blood he'd taken. It had been a long time since he'd let himself feed so heavily. But the burst of wild Power by the graveyard had caught him up in its frenzy, shattering his already weakened control. He still wasn't sure where the Power had come from. He had been watching the human girls from his place in the shadows when it had exploded from behind him, sending the girls fleeing. He had been caught between the fear that they would run into the river and the desire to probe this Power and find its source. In the end, he had followed *her*, unable to chance her getting hurt.

Something black had winged toward the

woods as the humans reached the sanctuary of the bridge, but even Stefan's night senses could not make out what it was. He had watched while *she* and the other two started in the direction of town. Then he had turned back to the graveyard.

It was empty now, purged of whatever had been there. On the ground lay a thin strip of silk that to ordinary eyes would have been gray in the dark. But he saw its true color, and as he crushed it between his fingers, bringing it slowly up to touch his lips, he could smell the scent of her hair.

Memory engulfed him. It was bad enough when she was out of sight, when the cool glow of her mind only teased at the edges of his consciousness. But to be in the same room with her at the school, to feel her presence behind him, to smell the heady fragrance of her skin all around him, was almost more than he could bear.

He had heard every soft breath she took, felt her warmth radiating against his back, sensed each throb of her sweet pulse. And eventually, to his horror, he had found himself giving in to it. His tongue had brushed back and forth over his canine teeth, enjoying the pleasure-pain that was building there, encouraging it. He'd breathed her smell into his nostrils deliberately, and let the visions come to him, imagining it all. How soft her neck would be, and how his lips would meet it with equal softness at first, planting tiny kisses here, and here, until he reached the yielding hollow of her throat. How he would nuzzle there, in the place where her heart beat so strongly against the delicate skin. And how at last his lips would part, would draw back from aching teeth now sharp as little daggers, and—

No. He'd brought himself out of the trance with a jerk, his own pulse beating raggedly, his body shaking. The class had been dismissed, movement was all around him, and he could only hope no one had been observing him too closely.

When she had spoken to him, he had been unable to believe that he had to face her while his veins burned and his whole upper jaw ached. He'd been afraid for a moment that his control would break, that he would seize her shoulders and take her in front of all of them. He had no idea how he'd gotten away, only that some time later he was channeling his energy into hard exercise, dimly aware that he must not use the Powers. It didn't matter; even without them he was in every way superior to the mortal boys who competed with him on the football field.

His sight was sharper, his reflexes faster, his muscles stronger. Presently a hand had clapped him on the back and Matt's voice had rung in his ears:

"Congratulations! Welcome to the team!"

Looking into that honest, smiling face, Stefan had been overcome with shame. If you knew what I was, you wouldn't smile at me, he'd thought grimly. I've won this competition of yours by deception. And the girl you love—you do love her, don't you?—is in my thoughts right now.

And she had remained in his thoughts despite all his efforts to banish her that afternoon. He had wandered to the graveyard blindly, pulled from the woods by a force he did not understand. Once there he had watched her, fighting himself, fighting the need, until the surge of Power had sent her and her friends running. And then he'd come home—but only after feeding. After losing control of himself.

He couldn't remember exactly how it had happened, how he'd let it happen. That flare of Power had started it, awakening things inside him best left sleeping. The hunting need. The craving for the chase, for the smell of fear and the savage triumph of the kill. It had been years —centuries—since he'd felt the need with such force. His veins had begun burning like fire. And all his thoughts had turned red: he could think of nothing else but the hot coppery taste, the primal vibrancy, of blood.

With that excitement still raging through him, he'd taken a step or two after the girls. What *might* have happened if he hadn't scented the old man was better not thought about. But as he reached the end of the bridge, his nostrils had flared at the sharp, distinctive odor of human flesh.

Human *blood.* The ultimate elixir, the forbidden wine. More intoxicating than any liquor, the steaming essence of life itself. And he was so tired of fighting the need.

There had been a movement on the bank under the bridge, as a pile of old rags stirred. And the next instant, Stefan had landed gracefully, catlike, beside it. His hand shot out and pulled the rags away, exposing a wizened, blinking face atop a scrawny neck. His lips drew back.

And then there was no sound but the feeding.

Now, as he stumbled up the main staircase of the boarding house, he tried not to think about it, and not to think about her—about the girl who tempted him with her warmth, her life. *She* had been the one he truly desired, but he must put a stop to that, he must kill any such thoughts before they were started from now on. For his sake, and for her own. He was her worst nightmare come true, and she didn't even know it.

"Who's there? Is that you, boy?" a cracked voice called sharply. One of the second-story doors opened, and a gray head poked out.

"Yes, *signora*— Mrs. Flowers. I'm sorry if I disturbed you."

"Ah, it takes more than a creaky floorboard to disturb me. You locked the door behind you?"

"Yes, *signora*. You're . . . safe."

"That's right. We need to be safe here. You never know what might be out there in those woods, do you?" He looked quickly at the smiling little face surrounded by wisps of gray hair, the bright darting eyes. Was there a secret hidden in them?

"Good night, *signora*."

"Good night, boy." She shut the door.

In his own room he fell onto the bed and lay staring up at the low, slanting ceiling.

Usually he rested uneasily at night; it was not his natural sleeping time. But tonight he was tired. It took so much energy to face the sunlight, and the heavy meal only contributed to his lethargy. Soon, although his eyes did not close, he no longer saw the whitewashed ceiling above him.

Random scraps of memory floated through his mind. Katherine, so lovely that evening by the fountain, moonlight silvering her pale golden hair. How proud he had been to sit with her, to be the one to share her secret. . . .

"But can you never go out in sunlight?"

"I *can*, yes, as long as I wear this." She held up a small white hand, and the moonlight shone on the lapis ring there. "But the sun tires me so much. I have never been very strong."

Stefan looked at her, at the delicacy of her features and the slightness of her body. She was almost as insubstantial as spun glass. No, she would never have been strong.

"I was often ill as a child," she said softly, her eyes on the play of water in the fountain. "The last time, the surgeon finally said I would die. I remember Papa crying, and I remember lying in my big bed, too weak to move. Even breathing was too much effort. I was so sad to leave the world and so cold, so very cold." She shivered, and then smiled.

"But what happened?"

"I woke in the middle of the night to see Gudren, my maid, standing over my bed. And then she stepped aside, and I saw the man she had brought. I was frightened. His name was Klaus, and I'd heard the people in the village say he was evil. I cried out to Gudren to save me, but she just stood there, watching. When he put his mouth to my neck, I thought he was going to kill me."

She paused. Stefan was staring at her in horror and pity, and she smiled comfortingly at him. "It was not so terrible after all. There was a little pain at first, but that quickly went away. And then the feeling was actually pleasant. When he gave me of his own blood to drink, I felt stronger than I had for months. And then we waited out the hours together until dawn. When the surgeon came, he couldn't believe I was able to sit up and speak. Papa said it was a miracle, and he cried again from happiness." Her face clouded. "I will have to leave my papa sometime soon. One day he will realize that since that illness I have not grown an hour older."

"And you never will?"

"No. That is the wonder of it, Stefan!" She gazed up at him with childlike joy. "I will be young forever, and I will never die! Can you imagine?"

He could not imagine her as anything other than what she was now: lovely, innocent, perfect. "But—you did not find it frightening at first?"

"At first, a little. But Gudren showed me what to do. It was she who told me to have this ring made, with a gem that would protect me from sunlight. While I lay in bed, she brought me rich warm possets to drink. Later, she brought small animals her son trapped."

"Not . . . people?"

Her laughter rang out. "Of course not. I can get all I need in a night from a dove. Gudren says that if I wish to be powerful I should take human blood, for the life essence of humans is strongest. And Klaus used to urge me, too; he wanted to exchange blood again. But I tell Gudren I do not want power. And as for Klaus . . ." She stopped and dropped her eyes, so that heavy lashes lay on her cheek. Her voice was very soft as she continued. "I do not think it is a thing to be done lightly. I will take human blood only when I have found my companion, the one who will be by my side for all eternity." She looked up at him gravely.

Stefan smiled at her, feeling light-headed and bursting with pride. He could scarcely contain the happiness he felt at that moment.

But that was before his brother Damon had returned from the University. Before Damon had come back and seen Katherine's jewel-blue eyes.

On his bed in the low-roofed room, Stefan moaned. Then the darkness drew him in deeper and new images began to flicker through his mind.

They were scattered glimpses of the past that did not form a connected sequence. He saw them like scenes briefly illuminated by flashes of lightning. His brother's face, twisted into a mask of inhuman anger. Katherine's blue eyes sparkling and dancing as she pirouetted in her new white gown. The glimmer of white behind a lemon tree. The feel of a sword in his hand; Giuseppe's voice shouting from far away. The lemon tree. He must not go behind the lemon tree. He saw Damon's face again, but this time his brother was laughing wildly. Laughing on and on, a sound like the grate of broken glass. And the lemon tree was closer now. . . .

"Damon—Katherine—*no!*"

He was sitting bolt upright on his bed.

He ran shaking hands through his hair and steadied his breath.

A terrible dream. It had been a long time since he had been tortured by dreams like that; long, indeed, since he'd dreamed at all. The last few seconds played over and over again in his mind, and he saw again the lemon tree and heard again his brother's laughter.

It echoed in his mind almost *too* clearly. Suddenly, without being aware of a conscious decision to move, Stefan found himself at the open window. The night air was cool on his cheeks as he looked into the silvery dark.

"Damon?" He sent the thought out on a surge of Power, questing. Then he fell into absolute stillness, listening with all his senses.

He could feel nothing, no ripple of response. Nearby, a pair of night birds rose in flight. In the town, many minds were sleeping; in the woods, nocturnal animals went about their secret business.

He sighed and turned back into the room. Perhaps he'd been wrong about the laughter; perhaps he'd even been wrong about the menace in the graveyard. Fell's Church was still, and peaceful, and he should try to emulate it. He needed sleep.

* * *

September 5 (actually early September 6—about 1:00 a.m.)
Dear Diary,

I should go back to bed soon. Just a few minutes ago I woke up thinking someone was shouting, but now the house is quiet. So many strange things have happened tonight that my nerves are shot, I guess.

At least I woke up knowing exactly what I'm going to do about Stefan. The whole thing just sort of sprang into my mind. Plan B, Phase One, begins tomorrow.

Frances's eyes were blazing, and her cheeks were flushed with color as she approached the three girls at the table.

"Oh, Elena, you've got to hear this!"

Elena smiled at her, polite but not too intimate. Frances ducked her brown head. "I mean . . . can I join you? I've just heard the wildest thing about Stefan Salvatore."

"Have a seat," said Elena graciously. "But," she added, buttering a roll, "we're not really interested in the news."

"You—?" Frances stared. She looked at Meredith, then at Bonnie. "You guys are joking, right?"

"Not at all." Meredith speared a green bean

and eyed it thoughtfully. "We have other things on our minds today."

"Exactly," said Bonnie after a sudden start. "Stefan's old news, you know. Passé." She bent down and rubbed her ankle.

Frances looked at Elena appealingly. "But I thought you wanted to know all about him."

"Curiosity," Elena said. "After all, he *is* a visitor, and I wanted to welcome him to Fell's Church. But of course I have to be loyal to Jean-Claude."

"Jean-Claude?"

"Jean-Claude," said Meredith, raising her eyebrows and sighing.

"Jean-Claude," echoed Bonnie gamely.

Delicately, with thumb and forefinger, Elena drew a photo out of her backpack. "Here he is standing in front of the cottage where we stayed. Right afterward he picked me a flower and said . . . well"—she smiled mysteriously—"I shouldn't repeat it."

Frances was gazing at the photo. It showed a bronzed young man, shirtless, standing in front of a hibiscus bush and smiling shyly. "He's older, isn't he?" she said with respect.

"Twenty-one. Of course"—Elena glanced over her shoulder—"my aunt would never approve, so we're keeping it from her until I graduate. We have to write to each other secretly."

"How romantic," Frances breathed. "I'll never tell a soul, I promise. But about Stefan . . ."

Elena gave her a superior smile. "If," she said, "I am going to eat Continental, I prefer French to Italian every time." She turned to Meredith. "Right?"

"Mm-*hmm*. *Every* time." Meredith and Elena smiled knowingly at each other, then turned to Frances. "Don't you agree?"

"Oh, yes," said Frances hastily. "Me, too. Every time." She smiled knowingly herself and nodded several times as she got up and left.

When she was gone, Bonnie said piteously, "This is going to kill me. Elena, I am going to die if I don't hear the gossip."

"Oh, that? I can tell you," Elena replied calmly. "She was going to say there's a rumor going around that Stefan Salvatore is a narc."

"A *what!*" Bonnie stared, and then burst into laughter. "But that's ridiculous. What narc in the world would dress like that and wear dark glasses? I mean, he's done everything he can to draw attention to himself. . . ." Her voice trailed off, and her brown eyes widened. "But then, that may be *why* he does it. Who would ever suspect anybody so obvious? And he does live alone, and he's awfully secretive. . . . Elena! What if it's true?"

"It isn't," said Meredith.

"How do you know?"

"Because I'm the one who started it." At Bonnie's expression, she grinned and added: "Elena told me to."

"Ohhhh." Bonnie looked admiringly at Elena. "You're wicked. Can I tell people he's got a terminal disease?"

"No, you cannot. I don't want any Florence Nightingale types lining up to hold his hand. But you can tell people whatever you want about Jean-Claude."

Bonnie picked up the photograph. "Who was he really?"

"The gardener. He was crazy about those hibiscus bushes. He was also married, with two kids."

"Pity," said Bonnie seriously. "And you told Frances not to tell anyone about him. . . ."

"Right." Elena checked her watch. "Which means that by, oh, say two o'clock, it ought to be all over the school."

After school, the girls went to Bonnie's house. They were greeted at the front door by a shrill yapping, and when Bonnie opened the door, a very old, very fat Pekingese tried to escape. His name was Yangtze, and he was so spoiled that no one except Bonnie's mother could stand him. He nipped at Elena's ankle as she went by.

The living room was dim and crowded, with lots of rather fussy furniture and heavy curtains at the windows. Bonnie's sister Mary was there, unpinning a cap from her wavy red hair. She was just two years older than Bonnie, and she worked at the Fell's Church clinic.

"Oh, Bonnie," she said, "I'm glad you're back. Hello, Elena, Meredith."

Elena and Meredith said "hello." "What's the matter? You look tired," said Bonnie.

Mary dropped her cap on the coffee table. Instead of answering, she asked a question in return. "Last night when you came home so upset, where did you say you girls had been?"

"Down in the— Just down by Wickery Bridge."

"That's what I thought." Mary took a deep breath. "Now, you listen to me, Bonnie McCullough. Don't you *ever* go out there again, and especially not alone and at night. Do you understand?"

"But why not?" Bonnie asked, bewildered.

"Because last night somebody was attacked out there, that's why not. And do you know where they found him? *Right on the bank under Wickery Bridge.*"

Elena and Meredith stared at her in disbelief, and Bonnie clutched at Elena's arm. "Somebody was attacked under the bridge? But who was it? What happened?"

"I don't know. This morning one of the cemetery workers spotted him lying there. He was some homeless person, I guess, and he'd probably been sleeping under the bridge when he was attacked. But he was half dead when they brought him in, and he hasn't regained consciousness yet. He may die."

Elena swallowed. "What do you mean, attacked?"

"I mean," said Mary distinctly, "that his throat was nearly ripped out. He lost an incredible amount of blood. They thought it might have been an animal at first, but now Dr. Lowen says it was a person. And the police think whoever did it may be hiding in the cemetery." Mary looked at each of them in turn, her mouth a straight line. "So if you *were* there by the bridge—or in the cemetery, Elena Gilbert—then this person may have been there with you. Get it?"

"You don't have to scare us anymore," said Bonnie faintly. "We get the point, Mary."

"All right. Good." Mary's shoulders slumped, and she rubbed at the back of her neck wearily. "I've got to lie down for a while. I didn't mean to be crabby." She walked out of the living room.

Alone, the three girls looked at one another.

"It could have been one of us," said Meredith quietly. "Especially you, Elena; you went there alone."

Elena's skin was prickling, that same painfully alert feeling she'd had in the old graveyard. She could feel the chill of the wind and see the rows of tall tombstones all around her. Sunshine and Robert E. Lee had never seemed so far away.

"Bonnie," she said slowly, "did you see somebody out there? Is that what you meant when you said someone was waiting for me?"

In the dim room, Bonnie looked at her blankly. "What are you talking about? I didn't say that."

"Yes, you did."

"No, I didn't. I never said that."

"Bonnie," said Meredith, "we both heard you. You stared out at the old gravestones, and then you told Elena—"

"I don't know what you're talking about, and

I didn't say *anything*." Bonnie's face was pinched with anger, but there were tears in her eyes. "I don't want to talk about it anymore."

Elena and Meredith looked at one another helplessly. Outside, the sun went behind a cloud.

Six

September 26
Dear Diary,

I'm sorry it's been so long, and I can't really explain why I haven't written—except that there are so many things I feel frightened to talk about, even to you.

First, the most terrible thing happened. The day that Bonnie and Meredith and I were at the cemetery, an old man was attacked there, and almost killed. The police still haven't found the person who did it. People think the old man was crazy, because when he woke up he started raving about "eyes in the dark" and oak trees and things. But I remember what happened to us that night, and I wonder. It scares me.

Everyone was scared for a while, and all the kids had to stay inside after dark or go out in groups. But it's been about three weeks now, and no more attacks, so the excitement is dying down. Aunt Judith says it must have been another vagrant that did it. Tyler Smallwood's father even suggested that the old man might have done it to himself—though I would like to see somebody bite himself in the throat.

But mostly what I've been busy with is Plan B. As far as it goes, it's been going well. I've gotten several letters and a bouquet of red roses from "Jean-Claude" (Meredith's uncle is a florist), and everybody seems to have forgotten that I was ever interested in Stefan. So my social position's secure. Even Caroline hasn't been making any trouble.

In fact, I don't know what Caroline is doing these days, and I don't care. I never see her at lunch or after school anymore; she seems to have drawn away from her old crowd completely.

There's only one thing I do care about right now. Stefan.

Even Bonnie and Meredith don't realize how important he is to me. I'm afraid to tell them; I'm afraid they'll think I'm crazy. At school I wear a mask of calm and control, but on the inside—well, every day it just gets worse.

Aunt Judith has started to worry about me. She says I don't eat enough these days, and she's right. I can't seem to concentrate on my classes, or even on anything fun like the Haunted House fund-raiser. I can't concentrate on anything but him. And I don't even understand why.

He hasn't spoken to me since that horrible afternoon. But I'll tell you something strange. Last week in history class, I glanced up and caught him looking at me. We were sitting a few seats apart, and he was turned completely sideways in his desk, just looking. For a moment I felt almost frightened, and my heart started pounding, and we just stared at each other—and then he looked away. But since then it's happened twice more, and each time I felt his eyes on me before I saw them. This is the literal truth. I know it's not my imagination.

He isn't like any boy I've ever known.

He seems so isolated, so lonely. Even though it's his own choice. He's made quite a hit on the football team, but he doesn't hang around with any of the guys, except maybe Matt. Matt's the only one he talks to. He doesn't hang around with any girls, either, that I can see, so maybe the narc rumor is doing some good. But it's more like he's avoiding other people than they're avoiding him. He disappears in between classes and after football practice, and I've never once seen him in the cafeteria. He's never invited anybody to his room at the boarding house. He never visits the coffee shop after school.

So how can I ever get him someplace where he can't run from me? This is the real problem with Plan

B. Bonnie says, "Why not get stuck in a thunderstorm with him, so you have to huddle together to conserve body warmth?" And Meredith suggested that my car could break down in front of the boarding house. But neither of those ideas is practical, and I'm going insane trying to come up with something better.

Every day it's getting worse for me. I feel as if I were a clock or something, winding up tighter and tighter. If I don't find something to do soon, I'll—

I was going to say "die."

The solution came to her quite suddenly and simply.

She felt sorry about Matt; she knew he'd been hurt by the Jean-Claude rumor. He'd hardly spoken to her since the story had broken, usually passing her with a quick nod. And when she ran into him one day in an empty hall outside of Creative Writing, he wouldn't meet her eyes.

"Matt—" she began. She wanted to tell him that it wasn't true, that she would never have started seeing another boy without telling him first. She wanted to tell him that she'd never meant to hurt him, and that she felt terrible now. But she didn't know how to begin. Finally, she just blurted out, "I'm sorry!" and turned to go in to class.

"Elena," he said, and she turned back. He was looking at her now, at least, his eyes lingering on her lips, her hair. Then he shook his head as if to say the joke was on him. "Is this French guy for real?" he finally demanded.

"No," said Elena immediately and without hesitation. "I made him up," she added simply, "to show everybody I wasn't upset about—" She broke off.

"About Stefan. I get it." Matt nodded, looking both grimmer and somewhat more understanding. "Look, Elena, that *was* pretty lousy of him. But I don't think he meant it personally. He's that way with everybody—"

"Except you."

"No. He talks to me, sometimes, but not about anything personal. He never says anything about his family or what he does outside of school. It's like—like there's a wall around him that I can't get through. I don't think he'll ever let anybody get through that wall. Which is a damn shame, because I think that behind it he's miserable."

Elena pondered this, fascinated by a view of Stefan she'd never considered before. He always seemed so controlled, so calm and undisturbed. But then, she knew she seemed that way herself to other people. Was it possible that underneath he was as confused and unhappy as she was?

It was then that the idea came, and it was ridiculously simple. No complicated schemes, no thunderstorms or cars breaking down.

"Matt," she said, slowly, "don't you think it would be a good thing if somebody did get behind that wall? A good thing for Stefan, I mean? Don't you think that would be the best thing that could happen to him?" She looked up at him intensely, willing him to understand.

He stared at her a moment, then shut his eyes briefly and shook his head in disbelief. "Elena," he said, "you are incredible. You twist people around your little finger, and I don't think you even know you're doing it. And now you're going to ask me to do something to help you ambush Stefan, and I'm such a dumb sucker I might even agree to do it."

"You're not dumb, you're a gentleman. And I *do* want to ask you a favor, but only if you think it's right. I don't want to hurt Stefan, and I don't want to hurt you."

"Don't you?"

"*No.* I know how that must sound, but it's true. I only want—" She broke off again. How could she explain what she wanted when she didn't even understand it herself?

"You only want everybody and everything re-volving around Elena Gilbert," he said bitterly. "You only want everything you don't have."

Shocked, she stepped back and looked at him. Her throat swelled, and warmth gathered in her eyes.

"Don't," he said. "Elena, don't look like that. I'm sorry." He sighed. "All right, what is it I'm supposed to do? Hog-tie him and dump him on your doorstep?"

"No," said Elena, still trying to make the tears go back where they belonged. "I only wanted you to get him to come to the Homecoming Dance next week."

Matt's expression was odd. "You just want him to be at the dance."

Elena nodded.

"All right. I'm pretty sure he'll be there. And, Elena . . . there really isn't anybody but you I want to take."

"All right," said Elena after a moment. "And, well, thank you."

Matt's expression was still peculiar. "Don't thank me, Elena. It's nothing . . . really." She was puzzling over that when he turned away and walked down the hall.

* * *

"Hold still," said Meredith, giving Elena's hair a reproving twitch.

"I still think," said Bonnie from the window seat, "that they were both wonderful."

"Who?" Elena murmured absently.

"As if you didn't know," said Bonnie. "Those two guys of yours who pulled off the last-minute miracle at the game yesterday. When Stefan caught that last pass, I thought I was going to faint. Or throw up."

"Oh, *please*," said Meredith.

"And Matt—that boy is simply poetry in motion. . . ."

"And neither of them is mine," Elena said flatly. Under Meredith's expert fingers, her hair was becoming a work of art, a soft mass of twisted gold. And the dress was all right; the iced-violet color brought out the violet in her eyes. But even to herself she looked pale and steely, not softly flushed with excitement but white and determined, like a very young soldier being sent to the front lines.

Standing on the football field yesterday when her name was announced as Homecoming Queen, there had been only one thought in her mind. He *couldn't* refuse to dance with her. If he came to the dance at all, he couldn't refuse the

Homecoming Queen. And standing in front of the mirror now, she said it to herself again.

"Tonight anyone you want will be yours," Bonnie was saying soothingly. "And, listen, when you get rid of Matt, can I take him off and comfort him?"

Meredith snorted. "What's Raymond going to think?"

"Oh, *you* can comfort *him.* But, really, Elena, I like Matt. And once you home in on Stefan, your threesome is going to get a little crowded. So . . ."

"Oh, do whatever you want. Matt deserves some consideration." He's certainly not getting it from me, Elena thought. She still couldn't exactly believe what she was doing to him. But just now she couldn't afford to second-guess herself; she needed all her strength and concentration.

"There." Meredith put the last pin in Elena's hair. "Now look at us, the Homecoming Queen and her court—or part of it, anyway. We're beautiful."

"Is that the royal 'we'?" Elena said mockingly, but it was true. They *were* beautiful. Meredith's dress was a pure sweep of burgundy satin, gathered tight at the waist and pouring into folds from the hips. Her dark hair hung loose down her back. And Bonnie, as she stood up and joined the others in front of the mirror, was like a shimmering party favor in pink taffeta and black sequins.

As for herself . . . Elena scanned her image with an experienced eye and thought again, The dress is all right. The only other phrase that came to mind was *crystallized violets*. Her grandmother had kept a little jar of them, real flowers dipped in crystallized sugar and frozen.

They went downstairs together, as they had for every dance since the seventh grade—except that before, Caroline had always been with them. Elena realized with faint surprise that she didn't even know who Caroline was going with tonight.

Aunt Judith and Robert—soon to be Uncle Robert—were in the living room, along with Margaret in her pajamas.

"Oh, you girls all look lovely," said Aunt Judith, as fluttery and excited as if she were going to the dance herself. She kissed Elena, and Margaret held up her arms for a hug.

"You're pretty," she said with four-year-old simplicity.

Robert was looking at Elena, too. He blinked, opened his mouth, and closed it again.

"What's the matter, Bob?"

"Oh." He looked at Aunt Judith, seeming embarrassed. "Well, actually, it just occurred to me that Elena is a form of the name Helen. And for some reason I was thinking of Helen of Troy."

"Beautiful and doomed," said Bonnie happily.

"Well, yes," said Robert, not looking happy at all. Elena said nothing.

The doorbell rang. Matt was on the step, in his familiar blue sports coat. With him were Ed Goff, Meredith's date, and Raymond Hernandez, Bonnie's. Elena looked for Stefan.

"He's probably already there," said Matt, interpreting her glance. "Listen, Elena—"

But whatever he had been about to say was cut off in the chatter from the other couples. Bonnie and Raymond went with them in Matt's car, and kept up a constant stream of witticisms all the way to the school.

Music drifted out the open doors of the auditorium. As Elena stepped out of the car, a curious certainty rushed over her. Something was going to happen, she realized, looking at the square bulk of the school building. The peaceful low gear of the last few weeks was about to slip into high.

I'm ready, she thought. And hoped it was true.

Inside, it was a kaleidoscope of color and activity. She and Matt were mobbed the instant they came in, and compliments rained down on both of them. Elena's dress . . . her hair . . . her flowers. Matt was a legend in the making: another Joe Montana, a sure bet for an athletic scholarship.

In the dizzying whirl that should have been life and breath to her, Elena kept searching for one dark head.

Tyler Smallwood was breathing heavily on her, smelling of punch and Brut and Doublemint gum. His date was looking murderous. Elena ignored him in the hopes that he would go away.

Mr. Tanner passed by with a soggy paper cup, looking as if his collar was strangling him. Sue Carson, the other senior homecoming princess, breezed up and cooed over the violet dress. Bonnie was already out on the dance floor, shimmering under the lights. But nowhere did Elena see Stefan.

One more whiff of Doublemint and she was going to be sick. She nudged Matt and they escaped to the refreshment table, where Coach Lyman launched into a critique of the game. Couples and groups came up to them, spending a few minutes and then retreating to make room for the next in line. Just as if we really *were* royalty, thought Elena wildly. She glanced sideways to see if Matt shared her amusement, but he was looking fixedly off to his left.

She followed his gaze. And there, half concealed behind a cluster of football players, was the dark head she'd been looking for. Unmistakable, even in this dim light. A thrill went through her, more of pain than anything else.

"Now what?" said Matt, his jaw set. "The hog-tying?"

"No. I'm going to ask him to dance, that's all. I'll wait until we've danced first, if you want."

He shook his head, and she set out toward Stefan through the crowd.

Piece by piece, Elena registered information about him as she approached. His black blazer was of a subtly different cut than the other boys', more elegant, and he wore a white cashmere sweater under it. He stood quite still, not fidgeting, a little apart from the groups around him. And, although she could see him only in profile, she could see he wasn't wearing his glasses.

He took them off for football, of course, but she'd never seen him close up without them. It made her feel giddy and excited, as if this were a masquerade and the unmasking time had come.

She focused on his shoulder, the line of his jaw, and then he was turning toward her.

In that instant, Elena was aware that she was beautiful. It wasn't just the dress, or the way her hair was done. She was beautiful in herself: slender, imperial, a thing made of silk and inner fire. She saw his lips part slightly, reflexively, and then she looked up into his eyes.

"Hello." Was that her own voice, so quiet and self-assured? His eyes were green. Green as oak leaves in summer. "Are you having a good time?" she said.

I am now. He didn't say it, but she knew it was what he was thinking; she could see it in the way he stared at her. She had never been so sure of her power. Except that actually he didn't look as if he were having a good time; he looked stricken, in pain, as if he couldn't take one more minute of this.

The band was starting up, a slow dance. He was still staring at her, drinking her in. Those green eyes darkening, going black with desire. She had the sudden feeling that he might jerk her to him and kiss her hard, without ever saying a word.

"Would you like to dance?" she said softly. *I'm playing with fire, with something I don't understand,* she thought suddenly. And in that instant she realized that she was frightened. Her heart began to pound violently. It was as if those green eyes spoke to some part of her that was buried deep beneath the surface—and that part was screaming "danger" at her. Some instinct older than civilization was telling her to run, to flee.

She never moved. The same force that was terrifying her was holding her there. This is out of control, she thought suddenly. Whatever was happening here was beyond her understanding, was nothing normal or sane. But there was no stopping it now, and even while frightened she was reveling in it. It was the most intense moment she'd ever experienced with a boy, but nothing at all was happening. He was just gazing at her, as if hypnotized, and she was gazing back, while the energy shimmered between them like heat lightning. She saw his eyes go darker, defeated, and felt the wild leap of her own heart as he slowly stretched out one hand.

And then it all shattered.

"Why, Elena, how *sweet* you look," said a voice, and Elena's vision was dazzled with gold. It was Caroline, her auburn hair rich and glossy, her skin tanned to a perfect bronze. She was wearing a dress of pure gold lamé that showed an incredibly daring amount of that perfect skin. She slipped one bare arm through Stefan's and smiled lazily up at him. They were stunning together, like a couple of international models slumming at a high school dance, far more glamorous and sophisticated than anyone else in the room.

"And that little dress is so *pretty*," continued Caroline, while Elena's mind kept on running on automatic. That casually possessive arm linked with Stefan's told her everything: where Caroline had been at lunch these past weeks, what she had been up to all this time. "I told Stefan we simply had to stop by for a moment, but we're not going to stay long. So you don't mind if I keep him to myself for the dances, do you?"

Elena was strangely calm now, her mind a humming blank. She said no, of course she didn't mind, and watched Caroline move away, a symphony in auburn and gold. Stefan went with her.

There was a circle of faces around Elena; she turned from them and came up against Matt.

"You knew he was coming with her."

"I knew she wanted him to. She's been following him around at lunchtime and after school, and kind of forcing herself on him. But . . ."

"I see." Still held in that queer, artificial calm, she scanned the crowd and saw Bonnie coming toward her, and Meredith leaving her table. They'd seen, then. Probably everyone had. Without a word to Matt, she moved toward them, heading instinctively for the girls' rest room.

It was packed with bodies, and Meredith and Bonnie kept their remarks bright and casual while looking at her with concern.

"Did you see that dress?" said Bonnie, squeezing Elena's fingers secretly. "The front must be held on with superglue. And what's she going to wear to the next dance? Cellophane?"

"Handiwrap," said Meredith. She added in a low voice, "Are you okay?"

"Yes." Elena could see in the mirror that her eyes were too bright and that there was one spot of color burning on each cheek. She smoothed her hair and turned away.

The room emptied, leaving them in privacy. Bonnie was fiddling nervously with the sequined bow at her waist now. "Maybe it isn't such a bad thing after all," she said quietly. "I mean, you haven't thought about anything else but him in weeks. Nearly a month. And so maybe it's just for the best, and you can move on to other things now, instead of . . . well, chasing him."

Et tu, Brute? thought Elena. "Thank you so much for your support," she said aloud.

"Now, Elena, don't be like that," Meredith put in. "She isn't trying to hurt you, she just thinks—"

"And I suppose you think so, too? Well, that's fine. I'll just go out and find myself some other things to move on to. Like some other best friends." She left them both staring after her.

Outside, she threw herself into the whirl of color and music. She was brighter than she had ever been at any dance before. She danced with everyone, laughing too loudly, flirting with every boy in her path.

They were calling her to come up and be crowned. She stood on the stage, looking down on the butterfly-bright figures below. Someone gave her flowers; someone put a rhinestone tiara on her head. There was clapping. It all passed as if in a dream.

She flirted with Tyler because he was closest when she came off the stage. Then she remembered what he and Dick had done to Stefan, and she broke off one of the roses from her bouquet and gave it to him. Matt was looking on from the sidelines, his mouth tight. Tyler's forgotten date was almost in tears.

She could smell alcohol along with the mint on Tyler's breath now, and his face was red. His friends were around her, a shouting, laughing crowd, and she saw Dick pour something from a brown paper bag into his glass of punch.

She'd never been with this group before. They welcomed her, admiring her, the boys vying for her attention. Jokes flew back and forth, and Elena laughed even when they didn't make sense. Tyler's arm circled her waist, and she just laughed harder. Out of the corner of her eye she saw Matt shake his head and walk away. The girls were getting shrill, the boys rowdy. Tyler was nuzzling moistly at her neck.

"I've got an idea," he announced to the group, hugging Elena more tightly to him. "Let's go someplace more fun."

Somebody shouted, "Like where, Tyler? Your dad's house?"

Tyler was grinning, a big, boozy, reckless grin. "No, I mean someplace where we can leave our mark. Like the cemetery."

The girls squealed. The boys elbowed each other and faked punches.

Tyler's date was still standing outside the circle. "Tyler, that's crazy," she said, her voice high and thin. "You know what happened to that old man. I won't go there."

"Great, then, you stay here." Tyler fished keys out of his pocket and waved them at the rest of the crowd. "Who *isn't* afraid?" he said.

"Hey, I'm up for it," said Dick, and there was a chorus of approval.

"Me, too," said Elena, clear and defiant. She smiled up at Tyler, and he practically swung her off her feet.

And then she and Tyler were leading a noisy, roughhousing group out into the parking lot, where they were all piling into cars. And then Tyler was putting the top of his convertible down and she was climbing in, with Dick and a girl named Vickie Bennett squashing into the back seat.

"Elena!" somebody shouted, far away, from the lighted doorway at the school.

"Drive," she said to Tyler, taking off her tiara, and the engine growled to life. They burned rubber out of the parking lot, and the cool night wind blew into Elena's face.

Seven

Bonnie was on the dance floor, eyes shut, letting the music flow through her. When she opened her eyes for an instant, Meredith was beckoning from the sidelines. Bonnie thrust her chin out mutinously, but as the gestures became more insistent she rolled her eyes up at Raymond and obeyed. Raymond followed.

Matt and Ed were behind Meredith. Matt was scowling. Ed was looking uncomfortable.

"Elena just left," said Meredith.

"It's a free country," said Bonnie.

"She went with Tyler Smallwood," said Meredith. "Matt, are you sure you didn't hear where they were going?"

Matt shook his head. "I'd say she deserves whatever happens—but it's my fault, too, in a way," he said bleakly. "I guess we ought to go after her."

"Leave the *dance?*" Bonnie said. She looked at Meredith, who mouthed the words *you promised.* "I don't believe this," she muttered savagely.

"I don't know how we'll find her," said Meredith, "but we've got to try." Then she added, in a strangely hesitant voice, "Bonnie, *you* don't happen to know where she is, do you?"

"What? No, of course not; I've been dancing. You've heard of that, haven't you: what you go to a dance for?"

"You and Ray stay here," Matt said to Ed. "If she comes back, tell her we're out looking."

"And if we're going, we'd better go now," Bonnie put in ungraciously. She turned and promptly ran into a dark blazer.

"Well, excuse *me,*" she snapped, looking up and seeing Stefan Salvatore. He said nothing as she and Meredith and Matt headed for the door, leaving an unhappy-looking Raymond and Ed behind.

The stars were distant and ice-bright in the cloudless sky. Elena felt just like them. Part of her was laughing and shouting with Dick and Vickie and Tyler over the roar of the wind, but part of her was watching from far away.

Tyler parked halfway up the hill to the ruined church, leaving his headlights on as they all got out. Although there had been several cars behind them when they left the school, they appeared to be the only ones who'd made it all the way to the cemetery.

Tyler opened the trunk and pulled out a six-pack. "All the more for us." He offered a beer to Elena, who shook her head, trying to ignore the sick feeling in the pit of her stomach. She felt all wrong being here—but there was no way she was going to admit that now.

They climbed the flagstone path, the girls staggering in their high heels and leaning on the boys. When they reached the top, Elena gasped and Vickie gave a little scream.

Something huge and red was hovering just above the horizon. It took Elena a moment to realize it was actually the moon. It was as large and unrealistic as a prop in a science-fiction movie, and its bloated mass glowed dully with an unwholesome light.

"Like a big rotten pumpkin," said Tyler, and lobbed a stone at it. Elena made herself smile brilliantly up at him.

"Why don't we go inside?" Vickie said, pointing a white hand at the empty hole of the church doorway.

Most of the roof had fallen in, although the belfry was still intact, a tower stretching up high above them. Three of the walls were standing; the fourth was only knee-high. There were piles of rubble everywhere.

A light flared by Elena's cheek, and she turned, startled, to see Tyler holding a lighter. He grinned, showing strong white teeth, and said, "Want to flick my Bic?"

Elena's laughter was the loudest, to cover her uneasiness. She took the lighter, using it to illuminate the tomb in the side of the church. It was like no other tomb in the cemetery, although her father said he'd seen similar things in England. It looked like a large stone box, big enough for two people, with two marble statues lying in repose on the lid.

"Thomas Keeping Fell and Honoria Fell," said Tyler with a grand gesture, as if introducing them. "Old Thomas allegedly founded Fell's Church. Although actually the Smallwoods were also there at the time. My great-grandfather's great-great-grandfather lived in the valley by Drowning Creek—"

"—until he got eaten by wolves," said Dick, and he threw back his head in a wolf imitation. Then he belched. Vickie giggled. Annoyance crossed Tyler's handsome features, but he forced a smile.

"Thomas and Honoria are looking kind of

pale," said Vickie, still giggling. "I think what they need is a little color." She produced a lipstick from her purse and began to coat the white marble mouth of the woman's statue with waxy scarlet. Elena felt another sick twinge. As a child, she'd always been awed by the pale lady and the grave man who lay with their eyes closed, hands folded on their breasts. And, after her parents died, she'd thought of them as lying side by side like this down in the cemetery. But she held the lighter while the other girl put a lipstick mustache and clown's nose on Thomas Fell.

Tyler was watching them. "Hey, they're all dressed up with no place to go." He put his hands on the edge of the stone lid and leaned on it, trying to shift it sideways. "What do you say, Dick—want to give them a night out on the town? Like maybe right in the center of town?"

No, thought Elena, appalled, as Dick guffawed and Vickie shrieked with laughter. But Dick was already beside Tyler, getting braced and ready, the heels of his hands on the stone lid.

"On three," said Tyler, and counted, "One, two, *three.*"

Elena's eyes were fixed on the horrible clown-like face of Thomas Fell as the boys strained forward and grunted, muscles bunching under cloth. They couldn't budge the lid an inch.

"Damn thing must be attached somehow," said Tyler angrily, turning away.

Elena felt weak with relief. Trying to seem casual, she leaned against the stone lid of the tomb for support—and that was when it happened.

She heard the grinding of stone and felt the lid shift under her left hand all at once. It was moving away from her, making her lose her balance. The lighter went flying, and she screamed and screamed again, trying to keep her feet. She was falling into the open tomb, and an icy wind roared all around her. Screams rang in her ears.

And then she was outside and the moonlight was bright enough that she could see the others. Tyler had hold of her. She stared around her wildly.

"Are you crazy? What happened?" Tyler was shaking her.

"It moved! The lid moved! It slid open and—I don't know—I almost fell in. It was cold . . ."

The boys were laughing. "Poor baby's got the jitters," Tyler said. "C'mon, Dicky-boy, we'll check it out."

"Tyler, no—"

But they went inside anyway. Vickie hung in

the doorway, watching, while Elena shivered. Presently, Tyler beckoned her from the door.

"Look," he said when she reluctantly stepped back inside. He'd retrieved the lighter, and he held it above Thomas Fell's marble chest. "It still fits, snug as a bug in a rug. See?"

Elena stared down at the perfect alignment of lid and tomb. "It did move. I nearly fell into it. . . ."

"Sure, whatever you say, baby." Tyler wound his arms around her, clasping her to him backwards. She looked over to see Dick and Vickie in much the same position, except that Vickie, eyes shut, was looking as if she enjoyed it. Tyler rubbed a strong chin over her hair.

"I'd like to go back to the dance now," she said flatly.

There was a pause in the rubbing. Then Tyler sighed and said, "Sure, baby." He looked at Dick and Vickie. "What about you two?"

Dick grinned. "We'll just stay here a while." Vickie giggled, her eyes still shut.

"Okay." Elena wondered how they were going to get back, but she allowed Tyler to lead her out. Once outside, however, he paused.

"I can't let you go without one look at my grandfather's headstone," he said. "Aw, c'mon, Elena," he said as she started to protest, "don't hurt my feelings. You've got to see it; it's the family pride and joy."

Elena made herself smile, although her stomach felt like ice. Maybe if she humored him, he would get her out of here. "All right," she said, and started toward the cemetery.

"Not that way. This way." And the next moment, he was leading her down toward the old graveyard. "It's okay, honest, it's not far off the path. Look, there, you see?" He pointed to something that shone in the moonlight.

Elena gasped, muscles tightening around her heart. It looked like a person standing there, a giant with a round hairless head. And she didn't like being here at all, among the worn and leaning granite stones of centuries past. The bright moonlight cast strange shadows, and there were pools of impenetrable darkness everywhere.

"It's just the ball on top. Nothing to be scared of," said Tyler, pulling her with him off the path and up to the shining headstone. It was made of red marble, and the huge ball that surmounted it reminded her of the bloated moon on the horizon. Now that same moon shone down on them, as white as Thomas Fell's white hands. Elena couldn't contain her shivering.

"Poor baby, she's cold. Got to get her warmed up," said Tyler. Elena tried to push him away, but he was too strong, wrapping her in his arms, pulling her against him.

"Tyler, I want to go; I want to go right now. . . ."

"Sure, baby, we'll go," he said. "But we've got to get you warm first. Gosh, you're cold."

"Tyler, stop," she said. His arms around her had merely been annoying, restricting, but now with a sense of shock she felt his hands on her body, groping for bare skin.

Never in her life had Elena been in a situation like this, far away from any help. She aimed a spiked heel for his patent-leather instep, but he evaded her. "Tyler, *take your hands off me."*

"C'mon, Elena, don't be like that, I just want to warm you up all over. . . ."

"Tyler, let go," she choked out. She tried to wrench herself away from him. Tyler stumbled, and then his full weight was on her, crushing her into the tangle of ivy and weeds on the ground. Elena spoke desperately. "I'll kill you, Tyler. I mean it. *Get off me."*

Tyler tried to roll off, giggling suddenly, his limbs heavy and uncoordinated, almost useless. "Aw, c'mon, Elena, don' be mad. I was jus' warmin' you up. Elena the Ice Princess, warmin' up . . . You're gettin' warm now, aren' you?"

Then Elena felt his mouth hot and wet on her

face. She was still pinned beneath him, and his sloppy kisses were moving down her throat. She heard cloth tear.

"Oops," Tyler mumbled. "Sorry 'bout that."

Elena twisted her head, and her mouth met Tyler's hand, clumsily caressing her cheek. She bit it, sinking her teeth into the fleshy palm. She bit *hard,* tasting blood, hearing Tyler's agonized yowl. The hand jerked away.

"Hey! I said I was sorry!" Tyler looked aggrievedly at his maimed hand. Then his face darkened, as, still staring at it, he clenched the hand into a fist.

This is it, Elena thought with nightmare calmness. He's either going to knock me out or kill me. She braced herself for the blow.

Stefan had resisted coming into the cemetery; everything within him had cried out against it. The last time he'd been here had been the night of the old man.

Horror shifted through his gut again at the memory. He would have sworn that he had not drained the man under the bridge, that he had not taken enough blood to do harm. But everything that night after the surge of Power was muddled, confused. If there *had* been a surge of Power at all. Perhaps that had been his own imagination, or even his own doing. Strange things could happen when the need got out of control.

He shut his eyes. When he'd heard that the old man was hospitalized, near death, his shock had been beyond words. How *could* he have let himself get so far out of hand? To kill, almost, when he had not killed since . . .

He wouldn't let himself think about that.

Now, standing in front of the cemetery gate in the midnight darkness, he wanted nothing so much as to turn around and go away. Go back to the dance where he'd left Caroline, that supple, sun-bronzed creature who was absolutely safe because she meant absolutely nothing to him.

But he couldn't go back, because Elena was in the cemetery. He could sense her, and sense her rising distress. Elena was in the cemetery and in trouble, and he had to find her.

He was halfway up the hill when the dizziness hit. It sent him reeling, struggling on toward the church because it was the only thing he could keep in focus. Gray waves of fog swept through his brain, and he fought to keep moving. Weak, he felt so weak. And helpless against the sheer power of this vertigo.

He needed . . . to go to Elena. But he was

weak. He couldn't be . . . weak . . . if he were to help Elena. He needed . . . to . . .

The church door yawned before him.

Elena saw the moon over Tyler's left shoulder. It was strangely fitting that it would be the last thing she ever saw, she thought. The scream had caught in her throat, choked off by fear.

And then something picked Tyler up and threw him against his grandfather's headstone.

That was what it looked like to Elena. She rolled to the side, gasping, one hand clutching her torn dress, the other groping for a weapon.

She didn't need one. Something moved in the darkness, and she saw the person who had plucked Tyler off her. Stefan Salvatore. But it was a Stefan she had never seen before: that fine-featured face was white and cold with fury, and there was a killing light in those green eyes. Without even moving, Stefan emanated such anger and menace that Elena found herself more frightened of him than she had been of Tyler.

"When I first met you, I knew you'd never learned any manners," said Stefan. His voice was soft and cold and light, and somehow it made Elena dizzy. She couldn't take her eyes off him as he moved toward Tyler, who was shaking his head dazedly and starting to get up. Stefan moved like a dancer, every movement easy and precisely controlled. "But I had no idea that your character was quite so underdeveloped."

He hit Tyler. The larger boy had been reaching out one beefy hand, and Stefan hit him almost negligently on the side of the face, before the hand made contact.

Tyler flew against another headstone. He scrambled up and stood panting, his eyes showing white. Elena saw a trickle of blood from his nose. Then he charged.

"A *gentleman* doesn't force his company on anyone," said Stefan, and knocked him aside. Tyler went sprawling again, facedown in the weeds and briars. This time he was slower in getting up, and blood flowed from both nostrils and from his mouth. He was blowing like a frightened horse as he threw himself at Stefan.

Stefan grabbed the front of Tyler's jacket, whirling them both around and absorbing the impact of the murderous rush. He shook Tyler twice, hard, while those big beefy fists windmilled around him, unable to connect. Then he let Tyler drop.

"He doesn't insult a woman," he said. Tyler's face was contorted, his eyes rolling, but he grabbed for Stefan's leg. Stefan jerked him to his feet and shook him again, and Tyler went limp as a rag doll, his eyes rolling up. Stefan went on speaking, holding the heavy body upright and punctuating every word with a bone-wrenching shake. "And, above all, he does *not* hurt her. . . ."

"Stefan!" Elena cried. Tyler's head was snapping back and forth with every shake. She was frightened of what she was seeing; frightened of what Stefan might do. And frightened above all else of Stefan's voice, that cold voice that was like a rapier dancing, beautiful and deadly and utterly merciless. "Stefan, *stop.*"

His head jerked toward her, startled, as if he had forgotten her presence. For a moment he looked at her without recognition, his eyes black in the moonlight, and she thought of some predator, some great bird or sleek carnivore incapable of human emotion. Then understanding came to his face and some of the darkness faded from his gaze.

He looked down at Tyler's lolling head, then set him gently against the red marble tombstone. Tyler's knees buckled and he slid down the face of it, but to Elena's relief his eyes opened—or at least the left one did. The right was swelling to a slit.

"He'll be all right," said Stefan emptily.

As her fear ebbed, Elena felt empty herself. Shock, she thought. I'm in shock. I'll probably start screaming hysterically any minute now.

"Is there someone to take you home?" said Stefan, still in that chillingly deadened voice.

Elena thought of Dick and Vickie, doing God knew what beside Thomas Fell's statue. "No," she said. Her mind was beginning to work again, to take notice of things around her. The violet dress was ripped all the way down the front; it was ruined. Mechanically, she pulled it together over her slip.

"I'll drive you," said Stefan.

Even through the numbness, Elena felt a quick thrill of fear. She looked at him, a strangely elegant figure among the tombstones, his face pale in the moonlight. He had never looked so . . . so *beautiful* to her before, but that beauty was almost alien. Not just foreign, but inhuman, because no human could project that aura of power, or of distance.

"Thank you. That would be very kind," she said slowly. There was nothing else to do.

They left Tyler painfully getting to his feet by his ancestor's headstone. Elena felt another chill as they reached the path and Stefan turned toward Wickery Bridge.

"I left my car at the boarding house," he said. "This is the fastest way for us to get back."

"Is this the way you came?"

"No. I didn't cross the bridge. But it'll be safe."

Elena believed him. Pale and silent, he walked beside her without touching, except when he took off his blazer to put it around her bare shoulders. She felt oddly sure he would kill anything that tried to get at her.

Wickery Bridge was white in the moonlight, and under it the icy waters swirled over ancient rocks. The whole world was still and beautiful and cold as they walked through the oak trees to the narrow country road.

They passed fenced pastures and dark fields until they reached a long winding drive. The boarding house was a vast building of rust-red brick made from the native clay, and it was flanked with age-old cedars and maples. All but one of the windows were dark.

Stefan unlocked one of the double doors and they stepped into a small hallway, with a flight of stairs directly in front of them. The banister, like the doors, was natural light oak so polished that it seemed to glow.

They went up the stairs to a second-story landing that was poorly lit. To Elena's surprise,

Stefan led her into one of the bedrooms and opened what looked like a closet door. Through it she could see a very steep, very narrow stairway.

What a strange place, she thought. This hidden stairway buried deep in the heart of the house, where no sound from outside could penetrate. She reached the top of the stairs and stepped out into a large room that made up the whole third story of the house.

It was almost as dimly lit as the stairway, but Elena could see the stained wood floor and the exposed beams in the slanting ceiling. There were tall windows on all sides, and many trunks scattered among a few pieces of massive furniture.

She realized he was watching her. "Is there a bathroom where I—?"

He nodded toward a door. She took off the blazer, held it toward him without looking at him, and went inside.

Eight

Elena had gone into the bathroom dazed and numbly grateful. She came out angry.

She wasn't quite sure how the transformation had taken place. But sometime while she was washing the scratches on her face and arms, annoyed at the lack of a mirror and at the fact she'd left her purse in Tyler's convertible, she started *feeling* again. And what she felt was anger.

Damn Stefan Salvatore. So cold and controlled even while saving her life. Damn him for his politeness, and for his gallantry, and for the walls around him that seemed thicker and higher than ever.

She pulled the remaining bobby pins out of her hair and used them to fasten the front of her dress together. Then she ran through her loosened hair quickly with an engraved bone comb she found by the sink. She came out of the bathroom with her chin held high and her eyes narrowed.

He hadn't put his coat back on. He was standing by the window in his white sweater with bowed head, tense, waiting. Without lifting his head, he gestured to a length of dark velvet laid over the back of a chair.

"You might want to put that on over your dress."

It was a full-length cloak, very rich and soft, with a hood. Elena pulled the heavy material around her shoulders. But she was not mollified by the gift; she noticed that Stefan hadn't come any closer to her, or even looked at her while speaking.

Deliberately, she invaded his territorial space, pulling the cloak more tightly about her and feeling, even at that moment, a sensual appreciation of the way the folds fell about her, trailing behind her on the floor. She walked up to him and made an examination of the heavy mahogany dresser by the window.

On it lay a wicked-looking dagger with an ivory hilt and a beautiful agate cup mounted in silver. There were also a golden sphere with some sort of dial set into it and several loose gold coins.

She picked up one of the coins, partly because it was interesting and partly because she knew it would upset him to see her handling his things. "What's this?"

It was a moment before he answered. Then he said:

"A gold florin. A Florentine coin."

"And what's this?"

"A German pendant watch. Late fifteenth century," he said distractedly. He added, "Elena—"

She reached for a small iron coffer with a hinged lid. "What about this? Does it open?"

"No." He had the reflexes of a cat; his hand slapped over the coffer, holding the lid down. "That's private," he said, the strain obvious in his voice.

She noticed that his hand made contact only with the curving iron lid and not with her flesh. She lifted her fingers, and he drew back at once.

Suddenly, her anger was too great to hold in any longer. "Careful," she said savagely. "Don't touch me, or you might get a disease."

He turned away toward the window.

And yet even as she moved away herself, walking back to the center of the room, she could sense his watching her reflection. And she knew, suddenly, what she must look like to him, pale hair spilling over the blackness of the cape, one white hand holding the velvet closed at her throat. A ravaged princess pacing in her tower.

She tilted her head far back to look at the trapdoor in the ceiling, and heard a soft, distinct intake of breath. When she turned, his gaze was fixed on her exposed throat; the look in his eyes confused her. But the next moment his face hardened, closing her out.

"I think," he said, "that I had better get you home."

In that instant, she wanted to hurt him, to make him feel as bad as he'd made her feel. But she also wanted the truth. She was tired of this game, tired of scheming and plotting and trying to read Stefan Salvatore's mind. It was terrifying and yet a wonderful relief to hear her own voice saying the words she'd been thinking so long.

"Why do you hate me?"

He stared at her. For a moment he couldn't seem to find words. Then he said, "I don't hate you."

"You do," said Elena. "I know it's not . . . not good manners to say it, but I don't care. I know I should be grateful to you for saving me tonight, but I don't care about that, either. I

125

didn't ask you to save me. I don't know why you were even in the graveyard in the first place. And I certainly don't understand why you did it, considering the way you feel about me."

He was shaking his head, but his voice was soft. "I don't hate you."

"From the very beginning, you've avoided me as if I were . . . were some kind of leper. I tried to be friendly to you, and you threw it back in my face. Is that what a *gentleman* does when someone tries to welcome him?"

He was trying to say something now, but she swept on, heedless. "You've snubbed me in public time after time; you've humiliated me at school. You wouldn't be speaking to me now if it hadn't been a matter of life or death. Is that what it takes to get a word out of you? Does someone have to nearly be murdered?

"And even now," she continued bitterly, "you don't want me to get anywhere near you. What's the matter with you, Stefan Salvatore, that you have to live this way? That you have to build walls against other people to keep them out? That you can't trust anyone? *What's wrong with you?*"

He was silent now, his face averted. She took a deep breath and then straightened her shoulders, holding her head up even though her eyes were sore and burning. "And what's wrong with *me*," she added, more quietly, "that you can't even look at me, but you can let Caroline Forbes fall all over you? I have a right to know that, at least. I won't ever bother you again, I won't even talk to you at school, but I want to know the truth before I go. Why do you hate me so much, Stefan?"

Slowly, he turned and raised his head. His eyes were bleak, sightless, and something twisted in Elena at the pain she saw on his face.

His voice was still controlled—but barely. She could hear the effort it cost him to keep it steady.

"Yes," he said, "I think you do have a right to know. Elena." He looked at her then, meeting her eyes directly, and she thought, That bad? What could be as bad as that? "I don't hate you," he continued, pronouncing each word carefully, distinctly. "I've never hated you. But you . . . remind me of someone."

Elena was taken aback. Whatever she'd expected, it wasn't this. "I remind you of someone else you know?"

"Of someone I knew," he said quietly. "But," he added slowly, as if puzzling something out for himself, "you're not like her, really. She looked

127

like you, but she was fragile, delicate. Vulnerable. Inside as well as out."

"And I'm not."

He made a sound that would have been a laugh if there had been any humor in it. "No. You're a fighter. You are . . . yourself."

Elena was silent for a moment. She could not keep hold of her anger, seeing the pain on his face. "You were very close to her?"

"Yes."

"What happened?"

There was a long pause, so long that Elena thought he wasn't going to answer her. But at last he said, "She died."

Elena let out a tremulous breath. The last of her anger folded up and disappeared from under her. "That must have hurt terribly," she said softly, thinking of the white Gilbert headstone among the rye grass. "I'm so sorry."

He said nothing. His face had closed again, and he seemed to be looking far away at something, something terrible and heartbreaking that only he could see. But there was not just grief in his expression. Through the walls, through all his trembling control, she could see the tortured look of unbearable guilt and loneliness. A look so lost and haunted that she had moved to his side before she knew what she was doing.

"Stefan," she whispered. He didn't seem to hear her; he seemed to be adrift in his own world of misery.

She could not stop herself from laying a hand on his arm. "Stefan, I know how it can hurt—"

"You *can't* know," he exploded, all his quietness erupting into white rage. He looked down at her hand as if just realizing it was there, as if infuriated at her effrontery in touching him. His green eyes were dilated and dark as he shook her hand off, flinging a hand up to bar her from touching him again—

—and somehow, instead, he was holding her hand, his fingers tightly interlocked with hers, hanging on for dear life. He looked down at their locked hands in bewilderment. Then, slowly, his gaze moved from their clasping fingers to her face.

"Elena . . ." he whispered.

And then she saw it, the anguish shattering his gaze, as if he simply couldn't fight any longer. The defeat as the walls finally crumbled and she saw what was underneath.

And then, helplessly, he bent his head down to her lips.

* * *

"Wait—stop here," said Bonnie. "I thought I saw something."

Matt's battered Ford slowed, edging toward the side of the road, where brambles and bushes grew thickly. Something white glimmered there, coming toward them.

"Oh, my God," said Meredith. "It's Vickie Bennett."

The girl stumbled into the path of the headlights and stood there, wavering, as Matt hit the brakes. Her light-brown hair was tangled and in disarray, and her eyes stared glassily out of a face that was smudged and grimy with dirt. She was wearing only a thin white slip.

"Get her in the car," said Matt. Meredith was already opening the car door. She jumped out and ran up to the dazed girl.

"Vickie, are you all right? What happened to you?"

Vickie moaned, still looking straight ahead. Then she suddenly seemed to see Meredith, and she clutched at her, digging her nails into Meredith's arms.

"Get out of here," she said, her eyes filled with desperate intensity, her voice strange and thick, as if she had something in her mouth. "All of you—get out of here! It's coming."

"What's coming? Vickie, where is Elena?"

"Get out *now.* . . ."

Meredith looked down the road, then led the shaking girl back to the car. "We'll take you away," she said, "but you have to tell us what's happened. Bonnie, give me your wrap. She's freezing."

"She's been hurt," said Matt grimly. "And she's in shock or something. The question is, where are the others? Vickie, was Elena with you?"

Vickie sobbed, putting her hands over her face as Meredith settled Bonnie's iridescent pink wrap around her shoulders. "No . . . Dick," she said indistinctly. It seemed to hurt her to speak. "We were in the church . . . it was horrible. It came . . . like mist all around. Dark mist. And eyes. I saw its eyes in the dark there, burning. They burnt me. . . ."

"She's delirious," said Bonnie. "Or hysterical, or whatever you call it."

Matt spoke slowly and clearly. "Vickie, please, just tell us one thing. Where is Elena? What happened to her?"

"I don't *know.*" Vickie lifted a tear-stained face to the sky. "Dick and I—we were alone. We were . . . and then suddenly it was all around us. I couldn't run. Elena said the tomb had opened. Maybe that was where it came from. It was horrible. . . ."

"They were in the cemetery, in the ruined church," Meredith interpreted. "And Elena was with them. And look at this." In the overhead light, they could all see the deep fresh scratches running down Vickie's neck to the lace bodice of her slip.

"They look like animal marks," said Bonnie. "Like the marks of cat's claws, maybe."

"No cat got that old man under the bridge," said Matt. His face was pale, and muscles stood out in his jaw. Meredith followed his gaze down the road and then shook her head.

"Matt, we have to take her back first. We *have* to," she said. "Listen to me, I'm as worried about Elena as you are. But Vickie needs a doctor, and we need to call the police. We don't have any choice. We have to go back."

Matt stared down the road for another long moment, then let out his breath in a hiss. Slamming the door shut, he put the car into gear and turned it around, each motion violent.

All the way back to town, Vickie moaned about the eyes.

Elena felt Stefan's lips meet hers.

And . . . it was as simple as that. All questions answered, all fears put to rest, all doubts removed. What she felt was not merely passion, but a bruising tenderness and a love so strong it made her shake inside. It would have been frightening in its intensity, except that while she was with him, she could not be afraid of anything.

She had come home.

This was where she belonged, and she had found it at last. With Stefan, she was home.

He pulled back slightly, and she could feel that he was trembling.

"Oh, Elena," he whispered against her lips. "We can't—"

"We already have," she whispered, and drew him back down again.

It was almost as if she could hear his thoughts, could feel his feelings. Pleasure and desire raced between them, connecting them, drawing them closer. And Elena sensed, too, a wellspring of deeper emotions within him. He wanted to hold her forever, to protect her from all harm. He wanted to defend her from any evil that threatened her. He wanted to join his life with hers.

She felt the tender pressure of his lips on hers, and she could hardly bear the sweetness of it. *Yes*, she thought. Sensation rippled through her like waves on a still, clear pond. She was drowning in it, both the joy she sensed in Stefan and the delicious answering surge in herself. Stefan's love bathed her, shone through her, lighting every dark place in her soul like the sun. She trembled with pleasure, with love, and with longing.

He drew back slowly, as if he could not bear to part from her, and they looked into each other's eyes with wondering joy.

They did not speak. There was no need for words. He stroked her hair, with a touch so light that she could scarcely feel it, as if he was afraid she might break in his hands. She knew, then, that it had not been hatred that had made him avoid her for so long. No, it had not been hatred at all.

Elena had no idea how much later it was that they quietly went down the stairs of the boarding house. At any other time, she would have been thrilled to get into Stefan's sleek black car, but tonight she scarcely noticed it. He held her hand as they drove through the deserted streets.

The first thing Elena saw as they approached her house was the lights.

"It's the police," she said, finding her voice with some difficulty. It was odd to talk after being silent so long. "And that's Robert's car in the driveway, and there's Matt's," she said. She looked at Stefan, and the peace that had filled her suddenly seemed fragile. "I wonder what happened. You don't suppose Tyler's already told them . . . ?"

"Even Tyler wouldn't be that stupid," said Stefan.

He pulled up behind one of the police cars, and reluctantly Elena unclasped her hand from his. She wished with all her heart that she and Stefan could just be alone together, that they would never need to face the world.

But there was no help for it. They walked up the pathway to the door, which was open. Inside, the house was a blaze of lights.

Entering, Elena saw what seemed like dozens of faces turned toward her. She had a sudden vision of what she must look like, standing there in the doorway in the sweeping black velvet cloak, with Stefan Salvatore at her side. And then Aunt Judith gave a cry and was holding her in her arms, shaking her and hugging her all at once.

"Elena! Oh, thank God you're safe. But where have you been? And why didn't you call? Do you realize what you've put everyone through?"

Elena stared around the room in bewilderment. She didn't understand a thing.

"We're just glad to see you back," said Robert.

"I've been at the boarding house, with Stefan," she said slowly. "Aunt Judith, this is Stefan Salvatore; he rents a room there. He brought me back."

"Thank you," said Aunt Judith to Stefan over Elena's head. Then, pulling back to look at Elena, she said, "But your dress, your hair—what happened?"

"You don't know? Then Tyler didn't tell you. But then why are the police here?" Elena edged toward Stefan instinctively, and she felt him move closer to her in protection.

"They're here because Vickie Bennett was attacked in the cemetery tonight," said Matt. He and Bonnie and Meredith were standing behind Aunt Judith and Robert, looking relieved and a little awkward and more than a little tired. "We found her maybe two, three hours ago, and we've been looking for you ever since."

"*Attacked?*" said Elena, stunned. "Attacked by what?"

"Nobody knows," said Meredith.

"Well, now, it may be nothing to worry about," said Robert comfortingly. "The doctor said she'd had a bad scare, and that she'd been drinking. The whole thing may have been in her imagination."

"Those scratches weren't imaginary," said Matt, polite but stubborn.

"What scratches? What are you talking about?" Elena demanded, looking from one face to another.

"I'll tell you," said Meredith, and she explained, succinctly, how she and the others had found Vickie. "She kept saying she didn't know where you were, that she was alone with Dick when it happened. And when we got her back here, the doctor said he couldn't find anything conclusive. She wasn't really hurt except for the scratches, and they could have been from a cat."

"There were no other marks on her?" said Stefan sharply. It was the first time he'd spoken since entering the house, and Elena looked at him, surprised by his tone.

"No," said Meredith. "Of course, a cat didn't tear her clothes off—but Dick might have. Oh, and her tongue was bitten."

"*What?*" said Elena.

"Badly bitten, I mean. It must have bled a lot, and it hurts her to talk now."

Beside Elena, Stefan had gone very still. "Did she have any explanation for what happened?"

"She was hysterical," Matt said. "Really hysterical; she wasn't making any sense. She kept babbling about eyes and dark mist and not being able to run—which is why the doctor thinks maybe it was some sort of hallucination. But as far as anyone can make out, the facts are that she and Dick Carter were in the ruined church by the cemetery at about midnight, and that something came in and attacked her there."

Bonnie added, "It didn't attack Dick, which at least shows it had some taste. The police found him passed out on the church floor, and he doesn't remember a thing."

But Elena scarcely heard the last words. Something had gone terribly wrong with Stefan. She couldn't tell how she knew it, but she knew. He had stiffened as Matt finished speaking, and now, though he hadn't moved, she felt as if a great distance was separating them, as if she and he were on opposite sides of a rifting, cracking floe of ice.

He said, in the terribly controlled voice she had heard before in his room, "In the church, Matt?"

"Yes, in the ruined church," Matt said.

"And you're sure she said it was midnight?"

"She couldn't be positive, but it must have

been sometime around then. We found her not long after. Why?"

Stefan said nothing. Elena could feel the gulf between them widening. "Stefan," she whispered. Then, aloud, she said desperately, "Stefan, what is it?"

He shook his head. Don't shut me out, she thought, but he wouldn't even look at her. "Will she live?" he asked abruptly.

"The doctor said there was nothing much wrong with her," Matt said. "Nobody's even suggested she might die."

Stefan's nod was abrupt; then he turned to Elena. "I've got to go," he said. "You're safe now."

She caught his hand as he turned away. "Of course I'm safe," she said. "Because of you."

"Yes," he said. But there was no response in his eyes. They were shielded, dull.

"Call me tomorrow." She squeezed his hand, trying to convey what she felt under the scrutiny of all those watching eyes. She willed him to understand.

He looked down at their hands with no expression at all, then, slowly, back up at her. And then, at last, he returned the pressure of her fingers. "Yes, Elena," he whispered, his eyes clinging to hers. The next minute he was gone.

She took a deep breath and turned back to the crowded room. Aunt Judith was still hovering, her gaze fixed on what could be seen of Elena's torn dress underneath the cloak.

"Elena," she said, "what *happened?*" And her eyes went to the door through which Stefan had just left.

A sort of hysterical laughter surged up in Elena's throat, and she choked it back. "Stefan didn't do it," she said. "Stefan saved me." She felt her face harden, and she looked at the police officer behind Aunt Judith. "It was Tyler, Tyler Smallwood. . . ."

Nine

She was not the reincarnation of Katherine.

Driving back to the boarding house in the faint lavender hush before dawn, Stefan thought about that.

He'd said as much to her, and it was true, but he was only now realizing how long he'd been working toward that conclusion. He'd been aware of Elena's every breath and move for weeks, and he'd catalogued every difference.

Her hair was a shade or two paler than Katherine's, and her eyebrows and lashes were darker. Katherine's had been almost silvery. And she was taller than Katherine by a good handspan. She moved with greater freedom, too; the girls of this age were more comfortable with their bodies.

Even her eyes, those eyes that had transfixed

him with the shock of recognition that first day, were not really the same. Katherine's eyes had usually been wide with childlike wonder, or else cast down as was proper for a young girl of the late fifteenth century. But Elena's eyes met you straight on, looked at you steadily and without flinching. And sometimes they narrowed with determination or challenge in a way Katherine's never had.

In grace and beauty and sheer fascination, they were alike. But where Katherine had been a white kitten, Elena was a snow-white tigress.

As he drove past the silhouettes of maple trees, Stefan cringed from the memory that sprang up suddenly. He would not think about that, he would not let himself . . . but the images were already unreeling before him. It was as if the journal had fallen open and he could do no more than stare helplessly at the page while the story played itself out in his mind.

White, Katherine had been wearing white that day. A new white gown of Venetian silk with slashed sleeves to show the fine linen chemise underneath. She had a necklace of gold and pearls about her neck and tiny pearl drop earrings in her ears.

She had been so delighted with the new dress her father had commissioned especially for her.

She had pirouetted in front of Stefan, lifting the full, floor-length skirt in one small hand to show the yellow brocaded underskirt beneath. . . .

"You see, it is even embroidered with my initials. Papa had that done. *Mein lieber Papa* . . ." Her voice trailed off, and she stopped twirling, one hand slowly settling to her side. "But what is wrong, Stefan? You are not smiling."

He could not even try. The sight of her there, white and gold like some ethereal vision, was a physical pain to him. If he lost her, he did not know how he could live.

His fingers closed convulsively around the cool engraved metal. "Katherine, how can I smile, how can I be happy when . . ."

"When?"

"When I see how you look at Damon." There, it was said. He continued, painfully. "Before he came home, you and I were together every day. My father and yours were pleased, and spoke of marriage plans. But now the days grow shorter, summer is almost gone—and you spend as much time with Damon as you do with me. The only reason Father allows him to stay here is that you asked it. But *why* did you ask it, Katherine? I thought you cared for me."

Her blue eyes were dismayed. "I do care for you, Stefan. Oh, you know I do!"

"Then why intercede for Damon with my father? If not for you, he'd have thrown Damon out into the street. . . ."

"Which I'm sure would have pleased *you*, little brother." The voice at the door was smooth and arrogant, but when Stefan turned he saw that Damon's eyes were smoldering.

"Oh, no, that isn't true," said Katherine. "Stefan would never wish to see you hurt."

Damon's lip quirked, and he threw Stefan a wry glance as he moved to Katherine's side. "Perhaps not," he said to her, his voice softening slightly. "But my brother is right about one thing at least. The days grow shorter, and soon your father will be leaving Florence. And he will take you with him—unless you have a reason to stay."

Unless you have a husband to stay with. The words were unspoken, but they all heard them. The baron was too fond of his daughter to force her to marry against her will. In the end it would have to be Katherine's decision. Katherine's choice.

Now that the subject was broached, Stefan could not keep silent. "Katherine knows she must leave her father sometime soon—" he began, flaunting his secret knowledge, but his brother interrupted.

"Ah, yes, before the old man grows suspicious," Damon said casually. "Even the most doting of fathers must start to wonder when his daughter comes forth only at night."

Anger and hurt swept through Stefan. It was true, then; Damon knew. Katherine had shared her secret with his brother.

"Why did you tell him, Katherine? Why? What can you see in him: a man who cares for nothing but his own pleasure? How can he make you happy when he thinks only of himself?"

"And how can this *boy* make you happy when he knows nothing of the world?" Damon interposed, his voice razor-sharp with contempt. "How will he protect you when he has never faced reality? He has spent his life among books and paintings; let him stay there."

Katherine was shaking her head in distress, her jewel-blue eyes misted with tears.

"Neither of you understand," she said. "You are thinking that I can marry and settle here like any other lady of Florence. But I cannot be like other ladies. How could I keep a household of servants who will watch my every move? How could I live in one place where the people will see that the years do not touch me? There will never be a normal life for me."

She drew a deep breath and looked at them each in turn. "Who chooses to be my husband must give up the life of sunlight," she whispered. "He must choose to live under the moon and in the hours of darkness."

"Then *you* must choose someone who is not afraid of shadows," Damon said, and Stefan was surprised by the intensity of his voice. He had never heard Damon speak so earnestly or with so little affectation. "Katherine, look at my brother: will he be able to renounce the sunlight? He is too attached to ordinary things: his friends, his family, his duty to Florence. The darkness would destroy him."

"Liar!" cried Stefan. He was seething now. "I am as strong as you are, *brother*, and I fear nothing in the shadows or the sunlight either. And I love Katherine more than friends or family—"

"—or your duty? Do you love her enough to give that up as well?"

"Yes," Stefan said defiantly. "Enough to give up everything."

Damon gave one of his sudden, disturbing smiles. Then he turned back to Katherine. "It would seem," he said, "that the choice is yours alone. You have two suitors for your hand; will you take one of us or neither?"

Katherine slowly bowed her golden head. Then she lifted wet blue eyes to both of them.

"Give me until Sunday to think. And in the meantime, do not press me with questions."

Stefan nodded reluctantly. Damon said, "And on Sunday?"

"Sunday evening at twilight I will make my choice."

Twilight . . . the violet deep darkness of twilight . . .

The velvet hues faded around Stefan, and he came to himself. It was not dusk, but dawn, that stained the sky around him. Lost in his thoughts, he had driven up to the edge of the woods.

To the northwest he could see Wickery Bridge and the graveyard. New memory set his pulse pounding.

He had told Damon he was willing to give up everything for Katherine. And that was just what he had done. He had renounced all claim to the sunlight, and had become a creature of darkness for her. A hunter doomed to be forever hunted himself, a thief who had to steal life to fill his own veins.

And perhaps a murderer.

No, they had said the girl Vickie would not die. But his next victim might. The worst thing about this last attack was that he remembered nothing of it. He remembered the weakness, the overpowering need, and he remembered staggering through the church door, but nothing after. He'd come to his senses outside with Elena's scream echoing in his ears—and he had raced to her without stopping to think about what might have happened.

Elena . . . For a moment he felt a rush of pure joy and awe, forgetting everything else. Elena, warm as sunlight, soft as morning, but with a core of steel that could not be broken. She was like fire burning in ice, like the keen edge of a silver dagger.

But did he have the right to love her? His very feeling for her put her in danger. What if the next time the need took him Elena was the nearest living human, the nearest vessel filled with warm, renewing blood?

I will die before touching her, he thought, making a vow of it. Before I broach her veins, I will die of thirst. And I swear she will never know my secret. She will never have to give up the sunlight because of me.

Behind him, the sky was lightening. But before he left, he sent out one probing thought, with all the force of his pain behind it, seeking for some other Power that might be near. Searching for some other solution to what had happened in the church.

But there was nothing, no hint of an answer. The graveyard mocked him with silence.

Elena woke with the sun shining in her window. She felt, at once, as if she'd just recovered from a long bout of the flu, and as if it were Christmas morning. Her thoughts jumbled together as she sat up.

Oh. She hurt all over. But she and Stefan—that made everything right. That drunken slob Tyler . . . But Tyler didn't matter anymore. Nothing mattered except that Stefan loved her.

She went downstairs in her nightgown, realizing from the light slanting in the windows that she must have slept in very late. Aunt Judith and Margaret were in the living room.

"Good morning, Aunt Judith." She gave her surprised aunt a long, hard hug. "And good morning, pumpkin." She swept Margaret off her feet and waltzed around the room with her. "And—oh! Good morning, Robert." A little embarrassed at her exuberance and her state of undress, she put Margaret down and hurried into the kitchen.

Aunt Judith came in. Though there were dark circles under her eyes, she was smiling. "You seem in good spirits this morning."

"Oh, I am." Elena gave her another hug, to apologize for the dark circles.

"You know we have to go back to the sheriff's to talk to them about Tyler."

"Yes." Elena got juice out of the refrigerator and poured herself a glass. "But can I go over to Vickie Bennett's house first? I know she must be upset, especially since it sounds like not everybody believes her."

"Do you believe her, Elena?"

"Yes," she said slowly, "I do believe her. And, Aunt Judith," she added, coming to a decision, "something happened to me in the church, too. I thought—"

"Elena! Bonnie and Meredith are here to see you." Robert's voice sounded from the hallway.

The mood of confidence was broken. "Oh . . . send them in," Elena called, and took a sip of orange juice. "I'll tell you about it later," she promised Aunt Judith, as footsteps approached the kitchen.

Bonnie and Meredith stopped in the doorway, standing with unaccustomed formality.

Elena herself felt awkward, and waited until her aunt left the room again to speak.

Then she cleared her throat, her eyes fixed on a worn tile in the linoleum. She sneaked a quick glance up and saw that both Bonnie and Meredith were staring at that same tile.

She burst into laughter, and at the sound they both looked up.

"I'm too happy to even be defensive," Elena said, holding out her arms to them. "And I know I ought to be sorry about what I said, and I *am* sorry, but I just can't be all pathetic about it. I was terrible and I deserve to be executed, and now can we just pretend it never happened?"

"You *ought* to be sorry, running off on us like that," Bonnie scolded as the three of them joined in a tangled embrace.

"And with Tyler Smallwood, of all people," said Meredith.

"Well, I learned my lesson on that score," Elena said, and for a moment her mood darkened. Then Bonnie trilled laughter.

"And you scored the big one yourself—Stefan Salvatore! Talk about dramatic entrances. When you came in the door with him, I thought I was hallucinating. How did you *do* it?"

"I didn't. He just showed up, like the cavalry in one of those old movies."

"Defending your honor," said Bonnie. "What could be more thrilling?"

"I can think of one or two things," said Meredith. "But then, maybe Elena's got those covered, too."

"I'll tell you all about it," Elena said, releasing them and stepping back. "But first will you come over to Vickie's house with me? I want to talk to her."

"You can talk to *us* while you're dressing, and while we're walking, and while you're brushing your teeth for that matter," said Bonnie firmly. "And if you leave out one tiny detail, you're going to be facing the Spanish Inquisition."

"You see," said Meredith archly, "all Mr. Tanner's work has paid off. Bonnie now knows the Spanish Inquisition is not a rock group."

Elena was laughing with sheer ebullience as they went up the stairs.

Mrs. Bennett looked pale and tired, but invited them in.

"Vickie's been resting; the doctor said to keep her in bed," she explained, with a smile that trembled slightly. Elena, Bonnie, and Meredith crowded into the narrow hallway.

Mrs. Bennett tapped lightly at Vickie's door. "Vickie, sweetheart, some girls from school to see you. Don't keep her long," she added to Elena, opening the door.

"We won't," Elena promised. She stepped into a pretty blue-and-white bedroom, the others right behind her. Vickie was lying in bed propped up on pillows, with a powder-blue comforter drawn up to her chin. Her face was paper-white against it, and her heavy-lidded eyes stared straight ahead.

"That's how she looked last night," Bonnie whispered.

Elena moved to the side of the bed. "Vickie," she said softly. Vickie went on staring, but Elena thought her breathing changed slightly. "Vickie, can you hear me? It's Elena Gilbert." She glanced uncertainly at Bonnie and Meredith.

"Looks like they gave her tranquilizers," said Meredith.

But Mrs. Bennett hadn't said they'd given her any drugs. Frowning, Elena turned back to the unresponsive girl.

"Vickie, it's me, Elena. I just wanted to talk to you about last night. I want you to know that I believe you about what happened." Elena ignored the sharp glance Meredith gave her and continued. "And I wanted to ask you—"

"No!" It was a shriek, raw and piercing, torn from Vickie's throat. The body that had been as still as a wax figure exploded into violent action. Vickie's light-brown hair whipped across her cheeks as she tossed her head back and forth and her hands flailed at the empty air. "No! No!" she screamed.

"Do something!" Bonnie gasped. "Mrs. Bennett! Mrs. Bennett!"

Elena and Meredith were trying to hold Vickie on the bed, and she was fighting them. The shrieking went on and on. Then suddenly Vickie's mother was beside them, helping to hold her, pushing the others away.

"What did you do to her?" she cried.

Vickie clutched at her mother, calming down, but then the heavy-lidded eyes glimpsed Elena over Mrs. Bennett's shoulder.

"You're part of it! You're evil!" she screamed hysterically at Elena. "Keep away from me!"

Elena was dumbfounded. "Vickie! I only came to ask—"

"I think you'd better leave now. Leave us alone," said Mrs. Bennett, clasping her daughter protectively. "Can't you see what you're doing to her?"

In stunned silence, Elena left the room. Bonnie and Meredith followed.

"It must be drugs," said Bonnie once they were out of the house. "She just went completely nonlinear."

"Did you notice her hands?" Meredith said to Elena. "When we were trying to restrain her, I got hold of one of her hands. And it was cold as ice."

Elena shook her head in bewilderment. None of it made sense, but she *wouldn't* let it spoil her day. She wouldn't. Desperately, she searched her mind for something that would offset the experience, that would allow her to hold on to her happiness.

"*I* know," she said. "The boarding house."

"What?"

"I told Stefan to call me today, but why don't we walk over to the boarding house instead? It's not far from here."

"Only a twenty-minute walk," said Bonnie. She brightened. "At least we can finally see that room of his."

"Actually," said Elena, "I was thinking you two could wait downstairs. Well, I'll only get to see him for a few minutes," she added, defensively, as they looked at her. It was odd, perhaps, but she didn't want to share Stefan with her friends just yet. He was so new to her that he felt almost like a secret.

Their knock on the shining oak door was answered by Mrs. Flowers. She was a wrinkled little gnome of a woman with surprisingly bright black eyes.

"You must be Elena," she said. "I saw you and Stefan go out last night, and he told me your name when he came back."

"You saw us?" said Elena, startled. "I didn't see you."

"No, no you didn't," said Mrs. Flowers, and chuckled. "What a pretty girl you are, my dear," she added. "A very pretty girl." She patted Elena's cheek.

"Uh, thank you," said Elena uneasily. She didn't like the way those birdlike eyes were fixed on her. She looked past Mrs. Flowers to the stairs. "Is Stefan home?"

"He must be, unless he's flown off the roof!" said Mrs. Flowers, and chuckled again. Elena laughed politely.

"We'll stay down here with Mrs. Flowers," said Meredith to Elena, while Bonnie rolled her eyes in martyrdom. Hiding a grin, Elena nodded and mounted the stairs.

Such a strange old house, she thought again as she located the second stairway in the bedroom. The voices below were very faint from here, and as she went up the steps they faded entirely. She was wrapped in silence, and as she reached the dimly lit door at the top, she had the feeling she had entered some other world.

Her knocking sounded very timid. "Stefan?"

She could hear nothing from inside, but suddenly the door swung open. *Everyone must look pale and tired today,* thought Elena, and then she was in his arms.

Those arms tightened about her convulsively. "Elena. Oh, Elena . . ."

Then he drew back. It was just the way it had been last night; Elena could feel the chasm opening between them. She saw the cold, correct look gather in his eyes.

"No," she said, hardly aware that she spoke aloud. "I won't let you." And she pulled his mouth down to hers.

For a moment there was no response, and then he shuddered, and the kiss became searing. His fingers tangled in her hair, and the universe shrank around Elena. Nothing else existed but Stefan, and the feel of his arms around her, and the fire of his lips on hers.

A few minutes or a few centuries later they separated, both shaking. But their gaze remained connected, and Elena saw that Stefan's eyes were too dilated for even this dim light; there was only a thin band of green around the dark pupils. He looked dazed, and his mouth—that mouth!—was swollen.

"I think," he said, and she could hear the control in his voice, "that we had better be careful when we do that."

Elena nodded, dazed herself. Not in public, she was thinking. And not when Bonnie and Meredith were waiting downstairs. And not when they were absolutely alone, unless . . .

"But you can just hold me," she said.

How odd, that after that passion she could feel so safe, so peaceful, in his arms. "I love you," she whispered into the rough wool of his sweater.

She felt a quiver go through him. "Elena," he said again, and it was a sound almost of despair.

She raised her head. "What's wrong with that? What could possibly be wrong with that, Stefan? Don't you love me?"

"I . . ." He looked at her, helplessly—and they heard Mrs. Flowers's voice calling faintly from the bottom of the stairs.

"Boy! Boy! Stefan!" It sounded as if she were pounding on the banister with her shoe.

Stefan sighed. "I'd better go see what she

wants." He slipped away from her, his face unreadable.

Left alone, Elena folded her arms across her chest and shivered. It was so cold here. He ought to have a fire, she thought, eyes moving idly around the room to rest finally on the mahogany dresser she'd examined last night.

The coffer.

She glanced at the closed door. If he came back in and caught her . . . She really shouldn't—but she was already moving toward the dresser.

Think of Bluebeard's wife, she told herself. Curiosity killed *her*. But her fingers were on the iron lid. Her heart beating rapidly, she eased the lid open.

In the dim light, the coffer appeared at first to be empty, and Elena gave a nervous laugh. What had she expected? Love letters from Caroline? A bloody dagger?

Then she saw the thin strip of silk, folded over and over on itself neatly in one corner. She drew it out and ran it between her fingers. It was the apricot ribbon she'd lost the second day of school.

Oh, Stefan. Tears stung her eyes, and in her chest love welled up helplessly, overflowing.

That long ago? You cared about me that long ago? Oh, Stefan, I love you. . . .

And it doesn't matter if you can't say it to me, she thought. There was a sound outside the door, and she folded the ribbon quickly and replaced it in the coffer. Then she turned toward the door, blinking tears from her eyes.

It doesn't matter if you can't say it right now. I'll say it for both of us. And someday you'll learn.

Ten

October 7, about 8:00 a.m.
Dear Diary,

I'm writing this during trig class, and I just hope Ms. Halpern doesn't see me.

I didn't have time to write last night, even though I wanted to. Yesterday was a crazy, mixed-up day, just like the night of the Homecoming Dance. Sitting here in school this morning I almost feel like everything that happened this weekend was a dream. The bad things were so bad, but the good things were so very, very good.

I'm not going to press criminal charges against Tyler. He's suspended from school, though, and off the football team. So's Dick, for being drunk at the dance. Nobody is saying so, but I think a lot of people think he was responsible for what happened to Vickie. Bonnie's sister saw Tyler at the clinic yesterday, and she said he had two black eyes and his whole face was purple. I can't help worrying about what's going to happen when he and Dick get back to school. They have more reason than ever to hate Stefan now.

Which brings me to Stefan. When I woke up this morning I panicked, thinking "What if it all isn't true? What if it never happened, or if he's changed his mind?" And Aunt Judith was worried at breakfast because I couldn't eat again. But then when I got to school I saw him in the corridor by the office, and we just looked at each other. And I knew. Just before he turned away, he smiled, sort of wryly. And I understood that, too, and he was right, it was better not to go up to each other in a public hallway, not unless we want to give the secretaries a thrill.

We are very definitely together. Now I just have to find a way to explain all this to Jean-Claude. Ha-ha.

What I don't understand is why Stefan isn't as happy about it as I am. When we're with each other I can feel how he feels, and I know how much he wants me, how much he cares. There's an almost desperate hunger inside him when he kisses me, as if he wants to pull the soul out of my body. Like a black hole that

Still October 7, now about 2:00 p.m.

Well, a little break there because Miss Halpern

caught me. *She even started to read what I'd written out loud, but then I think the subject matter steamed her glasses up and she stopped. She was Not Amused. I'm too happy to care about minor things like flunking trigonometry.*

Stefan and I had lunch together, or at least we went off into a corner of the field and sat down with my lunch. He didn't even bother to bring anything, and of course as it turned out I couldn't eat either. We didn't touch each other much—we didn't—but we talked and looked at each other a lot. I want to touch him. More than any boy I've ever known. And I know he wants it, too, but he's holding back on me.

That's what I can't understand, why he's fighting this, why he's holding back. Yesterday in his room I found proof positive that he's been watching me from the beginning. You remember how I told you that on the second day of school Bonnie and Meredith and I were in the cemetery? Well, yesterday in Stefan's room I found the apricot ribbon I was wearing that day. I remember it falling out of my hand while I was running, and he must have picked it up and kept it. I haven't told him I know, because he obviously wants to keep it a secret, but that shows, doesn't it, that he cares about me?

I'll tell you someone else who is Not Amused. Caroline. Apparently she's been dragging him off into the photography room for lunch every day, and when he didn't show up today she went searching until she found us. Poor Stefan, he'd forgotten about her completely, and he was shocked at himself. Once she left —a nasty unhealthy shade of green, I might add—he told me how she'd attached herself to him the first week of school. She said she'd noticed he didn't really eat at lunch and she didn't either since she was on a diet, and why didn't they go someplace quiet and relax? He wouldn't really say anything bad about her (which I think is his idea of manners again, a gentleman doesn't do that), but he did say there was nothing at all between them. And for Caroline I think being forgotten was worse than if he'd thrown rocks at her.

I wonder why Stefan hasn't been eating lunch, though. It's strange in a football player.

Uh-oh. Mr. Tanner just walked by and I slammed my note pad over this diary just in time. Bonnie is snickering behind her history book, I can see her shoulders shaking. And Stefan, who's in front of me, looks as tense as if he's going to leap out of his chair any minute. Matt is giving me "you nut" looks and Caroline is glaring. I am being very, very innocent, writing with my eyes fixed on Tanner up front. So if this is a bit wobbly and messy, you'll understand why.

For the last month, I haven't really been myself. I haven't been able to think clearly or concentrate on anything but Stefan. There is so much I've left undone that I'm almost scared. I'm supposed to be in charge of decorations for the Haunted House and I haven't done one thing *about* it yet. Now I've got exactly three and a half weeks to get it organized— and I want to be with Stefan.

I could quit the committee. But that would leave Bonnie and Meredith holding the bag. And I keep remembering what Matt said when I asked him to get Stefan to come to the dance: "You want everybody and everything revolving around Elena Gilbert."

That isn't true. Or at least, if it has been in the past, I'm not going to let it be true anymore. I want —oh, this is going to sound completely stupid, but I want to be worthy of Stefan. I know he wouldn't let the guys on the team down just to suit his own convenience. I want him to be proud of me.

I want him to love me as much as I love him.

"Hurry up!" called Bonnie from the doorway of the gym. Beside her the high school janitor, Mr. Shelby, stood waiting.

Elena cast one last glance at the distant figures on the football field, then reluctantly crossed the blacktop to join Bonnie.

"I just wanted to tell Stefan where I was going," she said. After a week of being with Stefan, she still felt a thrill of excitement just saying his name. Every night this week he'd come to her house, appearing at the door around sunset, hands in pockets, wearing his jacket with the collar turned up. They usually took a walk in the dusk, or sat on the porch, talking. Although nothing was said about it, Elena knew it was Stefan's way of making sure they weren't alone together in private. Since the night of the dance, he'd made sure of that. Protecting her honor, Elena thought wryly, and with a pang, because she knew in her heart that there was more to it than that.

"He can live without you for one evening," said Bonnie callously. "If you get talking to him you'll never get away, and I'd *like* to get home in time for some kind of dinner."

"Hello, Mr. Shelby," said Elena to the janitor, who was still patiently waiting. To her surprise, he closed one eye in a solemn wink at her. "Where's Meredith?" she added.

"Here," said a voice behind her, and Meredith appeared with a cardboard box of file folders and note pads in her arms. "I've got the stuff from your locker."

"Is that all of you?" said Mr. Shelby. "All right, now, you gals leave the door shut and locked, you hear? That way nobody can get in."

Bonnie, about to enter, pulled up short.

"You're sure there's nobody *already* in?" she said warily.

Elena gave her a push between the shoulder blades. "Hurry up," she mimicked unkindly. "I want to get home in time for dinner."

"There's nobody inside," said Mr. Shelby, mouth twitching under his mustache. "But you gals yell if you want anything. I'll be around."

The door slammed shut behind them with a curiously final sound.

"Work," said Meredith resignedly, and put the box on the floor.

Elena nodded, looking up and down the big empty room. Every year the Student Council held a Haunted House as a fund-raiser. Elena had been on the decorating committee for the last two years, along with Bonnie and Meredith, but it was different being chairman. She had to make decisions that would affect everyone, and she couldn't even rely on what had been done in years past.

The Haunted House was usually set up in a lumberyard warehouse, but with the growing uneasiness about town it had been decided that the school gym was safer. For Elena, it meant rethinking the whole interior design, and with less than three weeks now until Halloween.

"It's actually pretty spooky here," said Meredith quietly. And there *was* something disturbing about being in the big closed room, Elena thought. She found herself lowering her voice.

"Let's measure it first," she said. They moved down the room, their footsteps echoing hollowly.

"All right," said Elena when they had finished. "Let's get to work." She tried to shake off her feeling of uneasiness, telling herself that it was ridiculous to feel unsettled in the school gym, with Bonnie and Meredith beside her and an entire football team practicing not two hundred yards away.

The three of them sat on the bleachers with pens and notebooks in hand. Elena and Meredith consulted the design sketches for previous years while Bonnie bit her pen and gazed around thoughtfully.

"Well, here's the gym," said Meredith, making a quick sketch in her notebook. "And here's where the people are going to have to come in. Now we could have the Bloody Corpse at the very end. . . . By the way, who's going to be the Bloody Corpse this year?"

"Coach Lyman, I think. He did a good job last year, and he helps keep the football guys in line." Elena pointed to their sketch. "Okay, we'll partition this off and make it the Medieval Torture Chamber. They'll go straight out of that and into the Room of the Living Dead. . . ."

"I think we should have druids," said Bonnie abruptly.

"Have what?" said Elena, and then, as Bonnie started to yell "*droo*-ids," she waved a quelling hand. "All right, all right, I remember. But why?"

"Because they're the ones who invented Halloween. Really. It started out as one of their holy days, when they would build fires and put out turnips with faces carved in them to keep evil spirits away. They believed it was the day when the line between the living and the dead was thinnest. And they were scary, Elena. They performed human sacrifices. We could sacrifice Coach Lyman."

"Actually, that's not a bad idea," said Meredith. "The Bloody Corpse could be a sacrifice. You know, on a stone altar, with a knife and pools of blood all around. And then when you get really close, he suddenly sits up."

"And gives you heart failure," said Elena, but she had to admit it *was* a good idea, definitely scary. It made her feel a little sick just thinking about it. All that blood . . . but it was only Karo syrup, really.

The other girls had gone quiet, too. From the boys' locker next door, they could hear the sound of water running and lockers banging, and over that indistinct voices shouting.

"Practice is over," murmured Bonnie. "It must be dark outside."

"Yes, and Our Hero is getting all washed up," said Meredith, cocking an eyebrow at Elena. "Want to peek?"

"I wish," said Elena, only half jokingly. Somehow, indefinably, the atmosphere in the room had darkened. Just at the moment she *did* wish she could see Stefan, could be with him.

"Have you heard anything more about Vickie Bennett?" she asked suddenly.

"Well," said Bonnie after a moment, "I did hear that her parents were getting her a psychiatrist."

"A shrink? Why?"

"Well . . . I guess they think that those things she told us were hallucinations or something. And I heard her nightmares are pretty bad."

"Oh," said Elena. The sounds from the boys' locker room were fading, and they heard an outside door slam. Hallucinations, she thought, hallucinations and nightmares. For some reason, she suddenly remembered that night in the

170

graveyard, that night when Bonnie had sent them all running from something none of them could see.

"We'd better get back to business," said Meredith. Elena shook herself out of her reverie and nodded.

"We . . . we could have a graveyard," Bonnie said tentatively, as if she'd been reading Elena's thoughts. "In the Haunted House, I mean."

"*No*," said Elena sharply. "No, we'll just stick with what we have," she added in a calmer voice, and bent over her pad again.

Once again there was no sound but the soft scratching of pens and the rustle of paper.

"Good," said Elena at last. "Now we only need to measure for the different partitions. Somebody's going to have to get in behind the bleachers. . . . What now?"

The lights in the gym had flickered and gone down to half power.

"Oh, *no*," said Meredith, exasperated. The lights flickered again, went out, and returned dimly once more.

"I can't read a thing," said Elena, staring at what now seemed to be a featureless piece of white paper. She looked up at Bonnie and Meredith and saw two white blobs of faces.

"Something must be wrong with the emergency generator," said Meredith. "I'll get Mr. Shelby."

"Can't we just finish tomorrow?" Bonnie said plaintively.

"Tomorrow's Saturday," said Elena. "And we were supposed to have this done last week."

"I'll get Shelby," said Meredith again. "Come on, Bonnie, you're going with me."

Elena began, "We could all go—" but Meredith interrupted.

"If we all go and we can't find him, then we can't get back in. Come on, Bonnie, it's only inside the school."

"But it's *dark* there."

"It's dark everywhere; it's nighttime. Come *on*; with two of us it'll be safe." She dragged an unwilling Bonnie to the door. "Elena, don't let anybody else in."

"As if you had to tell me," said Elena, letting them out and then watching them go a few paces down the hall. At the point at which they began to merge with the dimness, she stepped back inside and shut the door.

Well, this was a fine mess, as her mother used to say. Elena moved over to the cardboard box Meredith had brought and began stacking filing folders and notebooks back inside it. In this light she could see them only as vague shapes. There was no sound at all but her own breathing and the sounds she made. She was alone in the huge, dim room—

Someone was watching her.

She didn't know how she knew, but she was sure. Someone was behind her in the dark gymnasium, watching. *Eyes in the dark*, the old man had said. Vickie had said it, too. And now there were eyes on her.

She whirled quickly to face the room, straining her own eyes to see into the shadows, trying not even to breathe. She was terrified that if she made a sound the thing out there would get her. But she could see nothing, hear nothing.

The bleachers were dim, menacing shapes stretching out into nothingness. And the far end of the room was simply a featureless gray fog. Dark mist, she thought, and she could feel every muscle agonizingly tense as she listened desperately. Oh God, what was that soft whispering sound? It must be her imagination. . . . Please let it be her imagination.

Suddenly, her mind was clear. She had to get out of this place, *now*. There was real danger here, not just fantasy. Something was out there, something evil, something that wanted her. And she was all alone.

Something moved in the shadows.

Her scream froze in her throat. Her muscles were frozen, too, held motionless by her terror —and by some nameless force. Helplessly, she watched as the shape in the darkness moved out of the shadows and toward her. It seemed almost as if the darkness itself had come to life and was coalescing as she watched, taking on form—human form, the form of a young man.

"I'm sorry if I frightened you."

The voice was pleasant, with a slight accent she couldn't place. It didn't sound sorry at all.

Relief was so sudden and complete that it was painful. She slumped and heard her own breath sigh out.

It was only a guy, some former student or an assistant of Mr. Shelby's. An ordinary guy, who was smiling faintly, as if it had amused him to see her almost pass out.

Well . . . perhaps not quite ordinary. He was remarkably good-looking. His face was pale in the artificial twilight, but she could see that his features were cleanly defined and nearly perfect under a shock of dark hair. Those cheekbones were a sculptor's dream. And he'd been almost invisible because he was wearing black: soft black boots, black jeans, black sweater, and leather jacket.

He was still smiling faintly. Elena's relief turned to anger.

"How did you get in?" she demanded. "And what are you doing here? Nobody else is supposed to be in the gym."

"I came in the door," he said. His voice was soft, cultured, but she could still hear the amusement and she found it disconcerting.

"All the doors are locked," she said flatly, accusingly.

He raised his eyebrows and smiled. "Are they?"

Elena felt another quiver of fear, hairs lifting on the back of her neck. "They were supposed to be," she said in the coldest voice she could manage.

"You're angry," he said gravely. "I said I was sorry to frighten you."

"I wasn't frightened!" she snapped. She felt foolish in front of him somehow, like a child being humored by someone much older and more knowledgeable. It made her even angrier. "I was just startled," she continued. "Which is hardly surprising, what with you lurking in the dark like that."

"Interesting things happen in the dark . . . sometimes." He was still laughing at her; she could tell by his eyes. He had taken a step closer, and she could see that those eyes were unusual, almost black, but with odd lights in them. As if you could look deeper and deeper until you fell into them, and went on falling forever.

She realized she was staring. Why didn't the lights come on? She wanted to get out of here. She moved away, putting the end of a bleacher between them, and stacked the last folders into the box. Forget the rest of the work for tonight. All she wanted to do now was leave.

But the continuing silence made her uneasy. He was just standing there, unmoving, watching her. Why didn't he say something?

"Did you come looking for somebody?" She was annoyed with herself for being the one to speak.

He was still gazing at her, those dark eyes fixed on her in a way that made her more and more uncomfortable. She swallowed.

With his eyes on her lips, he murmured, "Oh, yes."

"What?" She'd forgotten what she'd asked. Her cheeks and throat were flushing, burning with blood. She felt so light-headed. If only he'd stop *looking* at her . . .

"Yes, I came here looking for someone," he repeated, no louder than before. Then, in one step, he moved toward her, so that they were separated only by the corner of one bleacher seat.

Elena couldn't breathe. He was standing so close. Close enough to touch. She could smell a faint hint of cologne and the leather of his jacket. And his eyes still held hers—she could not look away from them. They were like no eyes she had ever seen, black as midnight, the pupils dilated like a cat's. They filled her vision as he leaned toward her, bending his head down to hers. She felt her own eyes half close, losing focus. She felt her head tilt back, her lips part.

No! Just in time she whipped her head to the side. She felt as if she'd just pulled herself back from the edge of a precipice. *What am I doing?* she thought in shock. *I was about to let him kiss me. A total stranger, someone I met only a few minutes ago.*

But that wasn't the worst thing. For those few minutes, something unbelievable had happened. For those few minutes, she had forgotten Stefan.

But now his image filled her mind, and the longing for him was like a physical pain in her body. She wanted Stefan, wanted his arms around her, wanted to be safe with him.

She swallowed. Her nostrils flared as she breathed hard. She tried to keep her voice steady and dignified.

"I'm going to leave now," she said. "If you're looking for somebody, I think you'd better look somewhere else."

He was looking at her oddly, with an expression she couldn't understand. It was a mixture of annoyance and grudging respect—and something else. Something hot and fierce that frightened her in a different way.

He waited until her hand was on the doorknob to answer, and his voice was soft but serious, with no trace of amusement. "Perhaps I've already found her . . . Elena."

When she turned, she could see nothing in the darkness.

Eleven

Elena stumbled down the dim corridor, trying to visualize what was around her. Then the world suddenly flickered to brightness and she found herself surrounded by familiar rows of lockers. Her relief was so great that she almost cried out. She'd never have thought she would be so glad just to *see*. She stood for a minute looking around gratefully.

"Elena! What are you doing out here?"

It was Meredith and Bonnie, hurrying down the hall toward her.

"Where have you been?" she said fiercely.

Meredith grimaced. "We couldn't find Shelby. And when we finally did find him, he was asleep. I'm serious," she added at Elena's incredulous look. "Asleep. And then we couldn't get him to wake up. It wasn't until the lights went back on that he opened his eyes. Then we started back to you. But what are you doing *here?*"

Elena hesitated. "I got tired of waiting," she said as lightly as she could. "I think we've done enough work for one day, anyway."

"Now you tell us," said Bonnie.

Meredith said nothing, but she gave Elena a keen, searching look. Elena had the uncomfortable feeling that those dark eyes saw beneath the surface.

All that weekend and throughout the following week, Elena worked on plans for the Haunted House. There was never enough time to be with Stefan, and that was frustrating, but even more frustrating was Stefan himself. She could sense his passion for her, but she could also sense that he was fighting it, still refusing to be completely alone with her. And in many ways he was just as much a mystery to her as he had been when she first saw him.

He never spoke about his family or his life before coming to Fell's Church, and if she asked any questions he turned them aside. Once she had asked him if he missed Italy, if he was sorry he'd come here. And for an instant his eyes had lightened, the green sparkling like oak leaves reflected in a running stream. "How could I be sorry, when *you* are here?" he said, and kissed her in a way that put all inquiries out of her mind. In that moment, Elena had known what it was like to be completely happy. She'd felt his joy, too, and when he pulled back she had seen that his face was alight, as if the sun shone through it.

"Oh, Elena," he'd whispered.

The good times were like that. But he had kissed her less and less frequently of late, and she felt the distance between them widening.

That Friday, she and Bonnie and Meredith decided to sleep over at the McCulloughs'. The sky was gray and threatening to drizzle as she and Meredith walked to Bonnie's house. It was unusually chilly for mid-October, and the trees lining the quiet street had already felt the nip of cold winds. The maples were a blaze of scarlet, while the ginkgoes were radiant yellow.

Bonnie greeted them at the door with: "Everybody's gone! We'll have the whole house to ourselves until tomorrow afternoon, when my family gets back from Leesburg." She beckoned them inside, grabbing for the overfed Pekingese that was trying to get out. "No, Yangtze, stay in. Yangtze, no, don't! No!"

But it was too late. Yangtze had escaped and was dashing through the front yard up to the single birch tree, where he yapped shrilly up into the branches, rolls of fat on his back jiggling.

"Oh, what's he after *now?*" said Bonnie, putting her hands over her ears.

"It looks like a crow," said Meredith.

Elena stiffened. She took a few steps toward the tree, looking up into the golden leaves. And there it was. The same crow she had seen twice before. Perhaps three times before, she thought, remembering the dark shape winging up from the oak trees in the cemetery.

As she looked at it she felt her stomach clench in fear and her hands grow cold. It was staring at her again with its bright black eye, an almost human stare. That eye . . . where had she seen an eye like that before?

Suddenly all three girls jumped back as the crow gave a harsh croak and thrashed its wings, bursting out of the tree toward them. At the last moment it swooped down instead on the little dog, which was now barking hysterically. It came within inches of canine teeth and then soared back up again, flying over the house to disappear into the black walnut trees beyond.

The three girls stood frozen in astonishment. Then Bonnie and Meredith looked at each other, and the tension shattered in nervous laughter.

"For a moment I thought he was coming for us," said Bonnie, going over to the outraged Pekingese and dragging him, still barking, back into the house.

"So did I," said Elena quietly. And as she followed her friends inside, she did not join in the laughter.

Once she and Meredith had put their things away, however, the evening fell into a familiar pattern. It was hard to keep hold of her uneasiness sitting in Bonnie's cluttered living room beside a roaring fire, with a cup of hot chocolate in her hand. Soon the three of them were discussing the final plans for the Haunted House, and she relaxed.

"We're in pretty good shape," said Meredith at last. "Of course, we've spent so much time figuring out everyone else's costumes that we haven't even thought about our own."

"Mine's easy," said Bonnie. "I'm going to be a druid priestess, and I only need a garland of oak leaves in my hair and some white robes. Mary and I can sew it in one night."

"I think I'll be a witch," said Meredith

thoughtfully. "All that takes is a long black dress. What about you, Elena?"

Elena smiled. "Well, it was supposed to be a secret, but . . . Aunt Judith let me go to a dressmaker. I found a picture of a Renaissance gown in one of the books I used for my oral report, and we're having it copied. It's Venetian silk, ice blue, and it's absolutely beautiful."

"It sounds beautiful," Bonnie said. "And expensive."

"I'm using my own money from my parents' trust. I just hope Stefan likes it. It's a surprise for him, and . . . well, I just hope he likes it."

"What's Stefan going to be? Is he helping with the Haunted House?" said Bonnie curiously.

"I don't know," Elena said after a moment. "He doesn't seem too thrilled with the whole Halloween thing."

"It's hard to see him all wrapped up in torn sheets and covered with fake blood like the other guys," agreed Meredith. "He seems . . . well, too dignified for that."

"I know!" said Bonnie. "I know exactly what he can be, and he'll hardly have to dress up at all. Look, he's foreign, he's sort of pale, he has that wonderful brooding look. . . . Put him in tails and you've got a perfect Count Dracula!"

Elena smiled in spite of herself. "Well, I'll ask him," she said.

"Speaking of Stefan," said Meredith, her dark eyes on Elena's, "how are things going?"

Elena sighed, looking away into the fire. "I'm . . . not sure," she said at last, slowly. "There are times when everything is wonderful, and then there are other times when . . ."

Meredith and Bonnie exchanged a glance, and then Meredith spoke gently. "Other times when what?"

Elena hesitated, debating. Then she came to a decision. "Just a sec," she said, and got up and hurried up the stairs. She came back down with a small blue velvet book in her hands.

"I wrote some of it down last night when I couldn't sleep," she said. "This says it better than I could now." She found the page, took a deep breath, and began:

"*October 17*
"*Dear Diary,*
"*I feel awful tonight. And I have to share it with someone.*
"*Something is going wrong with Stefan and me. There is this terrible sadness inside him that I can't reach, and it's driving us apart. I don't know what to do.*

"I can't bear the thought of losing him. But he's so very unhappy about something, and if he won't tell me what it is, if he won't trust me that much, I don't see any hope for us.

"Yesterday when he was holding me I felt something smooth and round underneath his shirt, something on a chain. I asked him, teasingly, if it was a gift from Caroline. And he just froze and wouldn't talk anymore. It was as if he were suddenly a thousand miles away, and his eyes . . . there was so much pain in his eyes that I could hardly stand it."

Elena stopped reading and traced the last lines written in the journal silently with her eyes. *I feel as if someone has hurt him terribly in the past and he's never got over it. But I also think there's something he's afraid of, some secret he's afraid I'll find out. If I only knew what that was, I could prove to him that he can trust me. That he can trust me no matter what happens, to the end.*

"If only I knew," she whispered.

"If only you knew what?" said Meredith, and Elena looked up, startled.

"Oh—if only I knew what was going to happen," she said quickly, closing the diary. "I mean, if I knew we were going to break up eventually, I suppose I'd just want to get it over with. And if I knew it was going to turn out all right in the end, I wouldn't mind anything that happens now. But just going day after day without being sure is awful."

Bonnie bit her lip, then sat up, eyes sparkling. "I can show you a way to find out, Elena," she said. "My grandmother told me the way to find out who you're going to marry. It's called a dumb supper."

"Let me guess, an old druid trick," said Meredith.

"I don't know how old it is," said Bonnie. "My grandmother says there have always been dumb suppers. Anyway, it works. My mother saw my father's image when she tried it, and a month later they were married. It's easy, Elena; and what have you got to lose?"

Elena looked from Bonnie to Meredith. "I don't know," she said. "But, look, you don't really believe . . ."

Bonnie drew herself up with affronted dignity. "Are you calling my mother a liar? Oh, come on, Elena, there's no harm in trying. Why not?"

"What would I have to do?" said Elena doubtfully. She felt strangely intrigued, but at the same time rather frightened.

"It's simple. We have to get everything ready before the stroke of midnight. . . ."

* * *

Five minutes before midnight, Elena stood in the McCulloughs' dining room, feeling more foolish than anything else. From the backyard, she could hear Yangtze's frantic barking, but inside the house there was no sound except the unhurried tick of the grandfather clock. Following Bonnie's instructions, she had set the big black walnut table with one plate, one glass, and one set of silverware, all the time not saying a word. Then she had lit a single candle in a candleholder in the center of the table, and positioned herself behind the chair with the place setting.

According to Bonnie, on the stroke of midnight she was supposed to pull the chair back and invite her future husband in. At that point, the candle would blow out and she would see a ghostly figure in the chair.

Earlier, she'd been a little uneasy about this, uncertain that she wanted to see *any* ghostly figures, even of her husband-to-be. But just now the whole thing seemed silly and harmless. As the clock began to chime, she straightened up and got a better grip on the chair back. Bonnie had told her not to let go until the ceremony was over.

Oh, this *was* silly. Maybe she wouldn't say the

words . . . but when the clock started to toll out the hour, she heard herself speaking.

"Come in," she said self-consciously to the empty room, drawing out the chair. "Come in, come in . . ."

The candle went out.

Elena started in the sudden darkness. She'd felt the wind, a cold gust that had blown out the candle. It came from the French doors behind her, and she turned quickly, one hand still on the chair. She would have sworn those doors were shut.

Something moved in the darkness.

Terror washed through Elena, sweeping away her self-consciousness and any trace of amusement. Oh, God, what had she done, what had she brought on herself? Her heart contracted and she felt as if she had been plunged, without warning, into her most dreadful nightmare. It was not only dark but utterly silent; there was nothing to see and nothing to hear, and she was falling . . .

"Allow me," said a voice, and a bright flame sputtered in the darkness.

For a terrible, sickening instant she thought it was Tyler, remembering his lighter in the ruined church on the hill. But as the candle on the table sprang to life, she saw the pale, long-fingered hand that held it. Not Tyler's beefy red fist. She thought for an instant it was Stefan's, and then her eyes lifted to the face.

"You!" she said, astounded. "What do you think you're *doing* here?" She looked from him to the French doors, which were indeed open, showing the side lawn. "Do you always just walk into other people's houses uninvited?"

"But you asked me to come in." His voice was as she remembered it, quiet, ironical and amused. She remembered the smile, too. "Thank you," he added, and gracefully sat down in the chair she had drawn out.

She snatched her hand off the back. "I wasn't inviting *you*," she said helplessly, caught between indignation and embarrassment. "What were you doing hanging around outside Bonnie's house?"

He smiled. In the candlelight, his black hair shone almost like liquid, too soft and fine for human hair. His face was very pale, but at the same time utterly compelling. And his eyes caught her own and held them.

" 'Helen, thy beauty is to me/Like those Nicean barks of yore/That gently, over a perfumed sea . . .' "

"I think you'd better leave now." She didn't want him to talk anymore. His voice did strange things to her, made her feel oddly weak, started a melting in her stomach. "You shouldn't be here. Please." She reached for the candle, meaning to take it and leave him, fighting off the dizziness that threatened to overcome her.

But before she could grasp it, he did something extraordinary. He caught her reaching hand, not roughly but gently, and held it in his cool slender fingers. Then he turned her hand over, bent his dark head, and kissed her palm.

"Don't . . ." whispered Elena, stunned.

"Come with me," he said, and looked up into her eyes.

"Please don't . . ." she whispered again, the world swimming around her. He was mad; what was he talking about? Come with him where? But she felt so dizzy, so faint.

He was standing, supporting her. She leaned against him, felt those cool fingers on the first button of the shirt at her throat. "Please, no . . ."

"It's all right. You'll see." He pulled the shirt away from her neck, his other hand behind her head.

"*No.*" Suddenly, strength returned to her, and she jerked away from him, stumbling against the chair. "I told you to leave, and I meant it. Get out—now!"

For an instant, pure fury surged in his eyes, a dark wave of menace. Then they went calm and cold and he smiled, a swift, brilliant smile that he turned off again instantly.

"I'll leave," he said. "For the moment."

She shook her head and watched him go out the French doors without speaking. When they had shut behind him, she stood in the silence, trying to get her breath.

The silence . . . but it shouldn't be silent. She turned toward the grandfather clock in bewilderment and saw that it had stopped. But before she could examine it closely, she heard Meredith's and Bonnie's raised voices.

She hurried out into the hall, feeling the unaccustomed weakness in her legs, pulling her shirt back up and buttoning it. The back door was open, and she could see two figures outside, stooping over something on the lawn.

"Bonnie? Meredith? What's wrong?"

Bonnie looked up as Elena reached them. Her eyes were filled with tears. "Oh, Elena, he's dead."

With a chill of horror, Elena stared down at the little bundle at Bonnie's feet. It was the Pekingese, lying very stiffly on his side, eyes open. "Oh, *Bonnie*," she said.

"He was old," said Bonnie, "but I never expected him to go this quickly. Just a little while ago, he was barking."

"I think we'd better go inside," said Meredith, and Elena looked up at her and nodded. Tonight was not a night to be out in the dark. It was not a night to invite things inside, either. She knew that now, although she still didn't understand what had happened.

It was when they got back in the living room that she found her diary was missing.

Stefan lifted his head from the velvet-soft neck of the doe. The woods were filled with night noises, and he couldn't be sure which had disturbed him.

With the Power of his mind distracted, the deer roused from its trance. He felt muscles quiver as she tried to get her feet under her.

Go, then, he thought, sitting back and releasing her entirely. With a twist and a heave, she was up and running.

He'd had enough. Fastidious, he licked at the corners of his mouth, feeling his canine teeth retract and blunt, oversensitive as always after a prolonged feed. It was hard to know what enough was anymore. There had been no spells of dizziness since the one beside the church, but he lived in fear of their return.

He lived in one specific fear: that he would come to his senses one day, his mind reeling with confusion, to find Elena's graceful body limp in his arms, her slim throat marked with two red wounds, her heart stilled forever.

That was what he had to look forward to.

The blood lust, with all its myriad terrors and pleasures, was a mystery to him even now. Although he had lived with it every day for centuries, he still did not understand it. As a living human, he would no doubt have been disgusted, sickened, by the thought of drinking the rich warm stuff directly from a breathing body. That is, if someone had proposed such a thing to him in so many words.

But no words had been used that night, the night Katherine had changed him.

Even after all these years, the memory was clear. He had been asleep when she appeared in his chamber, moving as softly as a vision or a ghost. He had been asleep, alone. . . .

She was wearing a fine linen shift when she came to him.

It was the night before the day she had named, the day when she would announce her choice. And she came to him.

A white hand parted the curtains around his

bed, and Stefan woke from sleep, sitting up in alarm. When he saw her, pale golden hair gleaming about her shoulders, blue eyes lost in shadow, he was struck silent with amazement.

And with love. He had never seen anything more beautiful in his life. He trembled and tried to speak, but she put two cool fingers over his lips.

"Hush," she whispered, and the bed sank under new weight as she got in.

His face flamed, his heart was thundering with embarrassment and with excitement. There had never been a woman in his bed before. And this was Katherine, Katherine whose beauty seemed to come from heaven, Katherine whom he loved more than his own soul.

And because he loved her, he made a great effort. As she slipped under the sheets, drawing so near to him that he could feel the cool freshness of night air in her thin shift, he managed to speak.

"Katherine," he whispered. "We—I can wait. Until we are married in the church. I will have my father arrange it next week. It—it will not be long. . . ."

"Hush," she whispered again, and he felt that coolness on his skin. He couldn't help himself; he put his arms around her, holding her to him.

"What we do now has nothing to do with that," she said, and reached out her slim fingers to stroke his throat.

He understood. And felt a flash of fear, which disappeared as her fingers went on stroking. He wanted this, wanted anything that would let him be with Katherine.

"Lie back, my love," she whispered.

My love. The words sang through him as he lay back on the pillow, tilting his chin back so that his throat was exposed. His fear was gone, replaced by a happiness so great that he thought it would shatter him.

He felt the soft brush of her hair on his chest, and tried to calm his breathing. He felt her breath on his throat, and then her lips. And then her teeth.

There was a stinging pain, but he held himself still and made no sound, thinking only of Katherine, of how he wished to give to her. And almost at once the pain eased, and he felt the blood being drawn from his body. It was not terrible, as he had feared. It was a feeling of giving, of nurturing.

Then it was as if their minds were merging, becoming one. He could feel Katherine's joy in drinking from him, her delight in taking the warm blood that gave her life. And he knew she could feel his delight in giving. But reality was receding, the boundaries between dreams and waking becoming blurred. He could not think clearly; he could not think at all. He could only *feel*, and his feelings were spiraling up and up, carrying him higher and higher, breaking his last ties with earth.

Sometime later, without knowing how he had gotten there, he found himself in her arms. She was cradling him like a mother holding an infant child, guiding his mouth to rest on the bare flesh just above the low neck of her night shift. There was a tiny wound there, a cut showing dark against the pale skin. He felt no fear or hesitation, and when she stroked his hair encouragingly, he began to suck.

Cold and precise, Stefan brushed dirt off his knees. The human world was asleep, lost in stupor, but his own senses were knife-keen. He should have been sated, but he was hungry again; the memory had wakened his appetite. Nostrils flaring wide to catch the musky scent of fox, he began to hunt.

Twelve

Elena revolved slowly before the full-length mirror in Aunt Judith's bedroom. Margaret sat at the foot of the big four-poster bed, her blue eyes large and solemn with admiration.

"I wish I had a dress like that for trick-or-treat," she said.

"I like you best as a little white cat," said Elena, dropping a kiss between the white velvet ears attached to Margaret's headband. Then she turned to her aunt, who stood by the door with needle and thread ready. "It's perfect," she said warmly. "We don't have to change a thing."

The girl in the mirror could have stepped out of one of Elena's books on the Italian Renaissance. Her throat and shoulders were bare, and the tight bodice of the ice-blue dress showed off her tiny waist. The long, full sleeves were slashed so that the white silk of the chemise underneath showed through, and the wide, sweeping skirt just brushed the floor all around her. It was a beautiful dress, and the pale clear blue seemed to heighten the darker blue of Elena's eyes.

As she turned away, Elena's gaze fell on the old-fashioned pendulum clock above the dresser. "Oh, no—it's almost seven. Stefan will be here any minute."

"That's his car now," said Aunt Judith, glancing out the window. "I'll go down and let him in."

"That's all right," said Elena briefly. "I'll meet him myself. Good-bye, have a good time trick-or-treating!" She hurried down the stairs.

Here goes, she thought. As she reached for the doorknob, she was reminded of that day, nearly two months ago now, when she'd stepped directly into Stefan's path in European History class. She'd had this same feeling of anticipation, of excitement and tension.

I just hope this turns out better than that plan did, she thought. For the last week and a half, she'd pinned her hopes to this moment, to this night. If she and Stefan didn't come together tonight, they never would.

The door swung open, and she stepped back

with her eyes down, feeling almost shy, afraid to see Stefan's face. But when she heard his sharp indrawn breath, she looked up quickly—and felt her heart go cold.

He was staring at her in wonder, yes. But it was not the wondering joy she'd seen in his eyes that first night in his room. This was something closer to shock.

"You don't like it," she whispered, horrified at the stinging in her eyes.

He recovered swiftly, as always, blinking and shaking his head. "No, no, it's beautiful. You're beautiful."

Then why are you standing there looking as if you'd seen a ghost? she thought. Why don't you hold me, kiss me—something!

"You look wonderful," she said quietly. And it was true; he was sleek and handsome in the tux and cape he'd donned for his part. She was surprised he'd agreed to it, but when she'd made the suggestion he'd seemed more amused than anything else. Just now, he looked elegant and comfortable, as if such clothes were as natural as his usual jeans.

"We'd better go," he said, equally quiet and serious.

Elena nodded and went with him to the car, but her heart was no longer merely cold; it was ice. He was further away from her than ever, and she had no idea how to get him back.

Thunder growled overhead as they drove to the high school, and Elena glanced out of the car window with dull dismay. The cloud cover was thick and dark, although it hadn't actually begun to rain yet. The air had a charged, electric feel, and the sullen purple thunderheads gave the sky a nightmarish look. It was a perfect atmosphere for Halloween, menacing and otherworldly, but it woke only dread in Elena. Since that night at Bonnie's, she'd lost her appreciation for the eerie and uncanny.

Her diary had never turned up, although they'd searched Bonnie's house top to bottom. She still couldn't believe that it was really gone, and the idea of a stranger reading her most private thoughts made her feel wild inside. Because, of course, it had been stolen; what other explanation was there? More than one door had been open that night at the McCullough house; someone could have just walked in. She wanted to *kill* whoever had done it.

A vision of dark eyes rose before her. That boy, the boy she'd almost given in to at Bonnie's house, the boy who'd made her forget Stefan. Was he the one?

She roused herself as they pulled up to the

school and forced herself to smile as they made their way through the halls. The gym was barely organized chaos. In the hour since Elena had left, everything had changed. Then, the place had been full of seniors: Student Council members, football players, the Key Club, all putting the finishing touches on props and scenery. Now it was full of strangers, most of them not even human.

Several zombies turned as Elena came in, their grinning skulls visible through the rotting flesh of their faces. A grotesquely deformed hunchback limped toward her, along with a corpse with livid white skin and hollow eyes. From another direction came a werewolf, its snarling muzzle covered with blood, and a dark and dramatic witch.

Elena realized, with a jolt, that she couldn't recognize half these people in their costumes. Then they were around her, admiring the ice-blue gown, announcing problems that had developed already. Elena waved them quiet and turned toward the witch, whose long dark hair flowed down the back of a tight-fitting black dress.

"What is it, Meredith?" she said.

"Coach Lyman's sick," Meredith replied grimly, "so somebody got Tanner to substitute."

"Mr. *Tanner?*" Elena was horrified.

"Yes, and he's making trouble already. Poor Bonnie's just about had it. You'd better get over there."

Elena sighed and nodded, then made her way along the twisting route of the Haunted House tour. As she passed through the grisly Torture Chamber and the ghastly Mad Slasher Room, she thought they had almost built *too* well. This place was unnerving even in the light.

The Druid Room was near the exit. There, a cardboard Stonehenge had been constructed. But the pretty little druid priestess who stood among the rather realistic-looking monoliths wearing white robes and an oak-leaf garland looked ready to burst into tears.

"But you've *got* to wear the blood," she was saying pleadingly. "It's part of the scene; you're a sacrifice."

"Wearing these ridiculous robes is bad enough," replied Tanner shortly. "No one informed me I was going to have to smear syrup all over myself."

"It doesn't really get on *you,*" said Bonnie. "It's just on the robes and on the altar. You're a sacrifice," she repeated, as if somehow this would convince him.

"As for that," said Mr. Tanner in disgust,

"the accuracy of this whole setup is highly suspect. Contrary to popular belief, the druids did *not* build Stonehenge; it was built by a Bronze Age culture that—"

Elena stepped forward. "Mr. Tanner, that isn't really the point."

"No, it wouldn't be, to you," he said. "Which is why you and your neurotic friend here are both failing history."

"That's uncalled for," said a voice, and Elena looked quickly over her shoulder at Stefan.

"Mister Salvatore," said Tanner, pronouncing the words as if they meant *Now my day is complete.* "I suppose you have some new words of wisdom to offer. Or are you going to give *me* a black eye?" His gaze traveled over Stefan, who stood there, unconsciously elegant in his perfectly tailored tux, and Elena felt a sudden shock of insight.

Tanner isn't really that much older than we are, she thought. He looks old because of that receding hairline, but I'll bet he's in his twenties. Then, for some reason, she remembered how Tanner had looked at Homecoming, in his cheap and shiny suit that didn't fit well.

I'll bet he never even made it to his own homecoming, she thought. And, for the first time, she felt something like sympathy for him.

Perhaps Stefan felt it, too, for although he stepped right up to the little man, standing face-to-face with him, his voice was quiet. "No, I'm not. I think this whole thing is getting blown out of proportion. Why don't . . ." Elena couldn't hear the rest, but he was speaking in low, calming tones, and Mr. Tanner actually seemed to be listening. She glanced back at the crowd that had gathered behind her: four or five ghouls, the werewolf, a gorilla, and a hunchback.

"All right, everything's under control," she said, and they dispersed. Stefan was taking care of things, although she was not sure how, since she could see only the back of his head.

The back of his head . . . For an instant, an image flashed before her of the first day of school. Of how Stefan had stood in the office talking to Mrs. Clarke, the secretary, and of how oddly Mrs. Clarke had acted. Sure enough, when Elena looked at Mr. Tanner now, he wore the same slightly dazed expression. Elena felt a slow ripple of disquiet.

"Come on," she said to Bonnie. "Let's go up front."

They cut straight through the Alien Landing Room and the Living Dead Room, slipping between the partitions, coming out in the first room where visitors would enter and be greeted by a werewolf. The werewolf had taken his head off and was talking to a couple of mummies and an Egyptian princess.

Elena had to admit that Caroline looked good as Cleopatra, the lines of that bronzed body frankly visible through the sheer linen sheath she wore. Matt, the werewolf, could hardly be blamed if his eyes kept straying downward from Caroline's face.

"How's it going here?" said Elena with forced lightness.

Matt started slightly, then turned toward her and Bonnie. Elena had scarcely seen him since the night of Homecoming, and she knew that he and Stefan had drawn apart, too. Because of her. And though Matt could hardly be blamed for *that*, either, she could tell how much it hurt Stefan.

"Everything's fine," said Matt, looking uncomfortable.

"When Stefan finishes with Tanner, I think I'll send him up here," Elena said. "He can help bring people in."

Matt lifted one shoulder indifferently. Then he said, "Finishes what with Tanner?"

Elena looked at him in surprise. She could

have sworn he'd been in the Druid Room a minute ago to see it. She explained.

Outside, thunder rumbled again, and through the open door Elena saw a flash light the night sky. There was another, louder clap of thunder a few seconds later.

"I hope it doesn't rain," Bonnie said.

"Yes," said Caroline, who had been standing silent while Elena spoke to Matt. "It would be such a *pity* if nobody came."

Elena glanced at her sharply and saw open hatred in Caroline's narrow, catlike eyes.

"Caroline," she said impulsively, "look. Can't you and I call it quits? Can't we forget what's happened and start over?"

Under the cobra on her forehead, Caroline's eyes widened and then slitted again. Her mouth twisted, and she stepped closer to Elena.

"I will *never* forget," she said, and then she turned and left.

There was a silence, Bonnie and Matt looking at the floor. Elena stepped over to the doorway to feel cool air on her cheeks. Outside she could see the field and the tossing branches of the oak trees beyond, and once again she was overcome with that strange feeling of foreboding. Tonight's the night, she thought wretchedly. Tonight's the night when it all happens. But what "it" was, she had no idea.

A voice sounded through the transformed gym. "All right, they're about to let the line in from the parking lot. Cut the lights, Ed!" Suddenly, gloom descended and the air was filled with groans and maniacal laughter, like an orchestra tuning up. Elena sighed and turned.

"Better get ready to start herding them through," she told Bonnie quietly. Bonnie nodded and disappeared into the darkness. Matt had donned his werewolf head, and was turning on a tape deck that added eerie music to the cacophony.

Stefan came around the corner, his hair and clothing melting into the darkness. Only his white shirtfront showed up clearly. "Everything worked out with Tanner," he said. "Is there anything else I can do?"

"Well, you could work here, with Matt, bringing people in. . . ." Elena's voice trailed off. Matt was bent over the tape deck, minutely adjusting the volume, not looking up. Elena looked at Stefan and saw his face was tight and blank. "Or you could go into the boys' locker room and be in charge of coffee and things for the workers," she finished tiredly.

"I'll go to the locker room," he said. As he

turned away, she noticed a slight faltering in his step.

"Stefan? Are you all right?"

"Fine," he said, recovering his balance. "A little tired, that's all." She watched him go, her chest feeling heavier every minute.

She turned to Matt, meaning to say something to him, but at that moment the line of visitors reached the door.

"Show's on," he said, and crouched in the shadows.

Elena moved from room to room, troubleshooting. In years before, she had enjoyed this part of the night the most, watching the gruesome scenes being acted out and the delicious terror of the visitors, but tonight there was a feeling of dread and tension underlying all her thoughts. Tonight's the night, she thought again, and the ice in her chest seemed to thicken.

A Grim Reaper—or at least that was what she supposed the hooded figure in black robes was —passed by her, and she found herself absentmindedly trying to remember if she had seen it at any of the Halloween parties. There was something familiar about the way the figure moved.

Bonnie exchanged a harassed smile with the tall, slender witch who was directing traffic into the Spider Room. Several junior high boys were slapping at the dangling rubber spiders and shouting and generally making a nuisance of themselves. Bonnie hustled them on into the Druid Room.

Here the strobe lights gave the scene a dream-like quality. Bonnie felt a grim triumph to see Mr. Tanner stretched out on the stone altar, his white robes heavily stained with blood, his eyes glaring at the ceiling.

"Cool!" shouted one of the boys, racing up to the altar. Bonnie stood back and grinned, waiting for the bloody sacrifice to rear up and scare the wits out of the kid.

But Mr. Tanner didn't move, even when the boy plunged a hand into the pool of blood by the sacrifice's head.

That's strange, Bonnie thought, hurrying up to prevent the kid from grabbing the sacrificial knife.

"Don't do that," she snapped, so he held up his gory hand instead, and it showed red in every sharp flash of the strobe. Bonnie felt a sudden irrational fear that Mr. Tanner was going to wait until she bent over him and then make *her* jump. But he just kept staring at the ceiling.

"Mr. Tanner, are you okay? Mr. Tanner? Mr. Tanner!"

Not a movement, not a sound. Not a flicker of those wide white eyes. Don't touch him, something in Bonnie's mind told her suddenly and urgently. Don't touch him don't touch him don't touch . . .

Under the strobe lights she saw her own hand move forward, saw it grasp Mr. Tanner's shoulder and shake it, saw his head flop bonelessly toward her. Then she saw his throat.

Then she began to scream.

Elena heard the screams. They were shrill and sustained and unlike any other sounds in the Haunted House, and she knew at once that they were no joke.

Everything after that was a nightmare.

Reaching the Druid Room at a run, she saw a tableau, but not the one prepared for visitors. Bonnie was screaming, Meredith holding her shoulders. Three young boys were trying to get out of the curtained exit, and two bouncers were looking in, blocking their way. Mr. Tanner was lying on the stone altar, sprawled out, and his face . . .

"He's dead," Bonnie was sobbing, the screams turning into words. "Oh, God, the blood's real, and he's dead. I *touched* him, Elena, and he's dead, he's really dead. . . ."

People were coming into the room. Someone else began screaming and it spread, and then everyone was trying to get out, pushing each other in panic, knocking into the partitions.

"Get the lights on!" Elena shouted, and heard the shout taken up by others. "Meredith, quick, get to a phone in the gym and call an ambulance, call the police. . . . Get those lights *on!*"

When the lights snapped on, Elena looked around, but she could see no adults, no one entitled to take charge of the situation. Part of her was ice-cold, her mind racing as it tried to think what to do next. Part of her was simply numb with horror. Mr. Tanner . . . She had never liked him, but somehow that only made it worse.

"Get all the kids out of here. Everybody but staff out," she said.

"No! Shut the doors! Don't let *anybody* out until the police get here," shouted a werewolf beside her, taking off his mask. Elena turned in astonishment at the voice and saw that it was not Matt, it was Tyler Smallwood.

He'd been allowed back in school only this week, and his face was still discolored from the beating he had taken at Stefan's hands. But his voice had the ring of authority, and Elena saw the bouncers close the exit door. She heard another door close across the gym.

Of the dozen or so people crowded into the Stonehenge area, Elena recognized only one as a worker. The rest were people she knew from school, but none she knew well. One of them, a boy dressed as a pirate, spoke to Tyler.

"You mean . . . you think somebody in here did it?"

"Somebody in here did it, all right," said Tyler. There was a queer, excited sound to his voice, as if he were almost enjoying this. He gestured to the pool of blood on the rock. "That's still liquid; it can't have happened too long ago. And look at the way his throat's cut. The killer must have done it with *that*." He pointed to the sacrificial knife.

"Then the killer might be here right now," whispered a girl in a kimono.

"And it's not hard to guess who it is," said Tyler. "Somebody who hated Tanner, who was always getting in arguments with him. Somebody who was arguing with him earlier tonight. I saw it."

So *you* were the werewolf in this room, thought Elena dazedly. But what were you doing here in the first place? You're not on staff.

"Somebody who has a history of violence," Tyler was continuing, his lips drawing back from his teeth. "Somebody who, for all we know, is a psychopath who came to Fell's Church just to kill."

"Tyler, what are you talking about?" Elena's dazed feeling had burst like a bubble. Furious, she stepped toward the tall, husky boy. "You're crazy!"

He gestured at her without looking at her. "So says his girlfriend—but maybe she's a little prejudiced."

"And maybe *you're* a little prejudiced, Tyler," said a voice from behind the crowd, and Elena saw a second werewolf pushing his way into the room. Matt.

"Oh, yeah? Well, why don't you tell us what *you* know about Salvatore? Where does he come from? Where's his family? Where did he get all that money?" Tyler turned to address the rest of the crowd. "Who knows *anything* about him?"

People were shaking their heads. Elena could see, in face after face, distrust blossoming. The distrust of anything unknown, anything different. And Stefan was different. He was the stranger in their midst, and just now they needed a scapegoat.

The girl in the kimono began, "I heard a rumor—"

"That's all anybody's heard, rumors!" Tyler said. "No one really *knows* a thing about him. But there's one thing I *do* know. The attacks in Fell's Church started the first week of school—*which was the week Stefan Salvatore came.*"

There was a swelling murmur at this, and Elena herself felt a shock of realization. Of course, it was all ridiculous, it was just a coincidence. But what Tyler was saying was true. The attacks had started when Stefan arrived.

"I'll tell you something else," shouted Tyler, gesturing at them to be quiet. "Listen to me! I'll tell you something else!" He waited until everyone was looking at him and then said slowly, impressively, "He was *in* the cemetery the night Vickie Bennett was attacked."

"Sure he was in the cemetery—rearranging your face," said Matt, but his voice lacked its usual strength. Tyler grabbed the comment and ran with it.

"Yes, and he almost killed me. And tonight somebody *did* kill Tanner. I don't know what *you* think, but *I* think he did it. I think he's the one!"

"But where is he?" shouted someone from the crowd.

Tyler looked around. "If he did it, he must still be here," he shouted. "Let's find him."

"Stefan hasn't done anything! Tyler—" cried Elena, but the noise from the crowd overrode her. Tyler's words were being taken up and repeated. *Find him . . . find him . . . find him.* Elena heard it pass from person to person. And the faces in the Stonehenge Room were filled with more than distrust now; Elena could see anger and a thirst for vengeance in them, too. The crowd had turned into something ugly, something beyond controlling.

"Where is he, Elena?" said Tyler, and she saw the blazing triumph in his eyes. He *was* enjoying this.

"I don't know," she said fiercely, wanting to hit him.

"He must still be here! Find him!" someone shouted, and then it seemed everyone was moving, pointing, pushing, at once. Partitions were being knocked down and shoved aside.

Elena's heart was pounding. This was no longer a crowd; it was a mob. She was terrified of what they would do to Stefan if they did find him. But if she tried to go warn him, she would lead Tyler right to him.

She looked around desperately. Bonnie was still staring into Mr. Tanner's dead face. No help there. She turned to scan the crowd again, and her eyes met Matt's.

He was looking confused and angry, his blond hair ruffled up, cheeks flushed and sweaty. Elena put all her strength of will into a look of pleading.

Please, Matt, she thought. You can't believe all this. You know it isn't true.

But his eyes showed that he *didn't* know. There was a tumult of bewilderment and agitation in them.

Please, thought Elena, gazing into those blue eyes, willing him to understand. Oh, please, Matt, only you can save him. Even if you don't believe, please try to trust . . . please . . .

She saw the change come over his face, the confusion lifting as grim determination appeared. He stared at her another moment, eyes boring into hers, and nodded once. Then he turned and slipped into the milling, hunting crowd.

Matt knifed through the crowd cleanly until he got to the other side of the gym. There were some freshmen standing near the door to the boys' locker room; he brusquely ordered them

217

to start moving fallen partitions, and when their attention was distracted he jerked the door open and ducked inside.

He looked around quickly, unwilling to shout. For that matter, he thought, Stefan must have heard all the racket going on in the gym. He'd probably already cut out. But then Matt saw the black-clad figure on the white tile floor.

"Stefan! What happened?" For a terrible instant, Matt thought he was looking down on a second dead body. But as he knelt by Stefan's side, he saw movement.

"Hey, you're okay, just sit up slowly . . . easy. Are you all right, Stefan?"

"Yes," said Stefan. He didn't look okay, Matt thought. His face was dead white and his pupils were dilated hugely. He looked disoriented and sick. "Thank you," he said.

"You may not thank me in a minute. Stefan, you've got to get out of here. Can't you hear them? They're after you."

Stefan turned toward the gym, as if listening. But there was no comprehension on his face. "Who's after me? Why?"

"Everybody. It doesn't matter. What matters is that you've got to get out before they come in here." As Stefan continued simply to stare blankly, he added, "There's been another attack, this time on Tanner, Mr. Tanner. He's dead, Stefan, and they think you did it."

Now, at last, he saw understanding come to Stefan's eyes. Understanding and horror and a kind of resigned defeat that was more frightening than anything Matt had seen tonight. He gripped Stefan's shoulder hard.

"I *know* you didn't," he said, and at that moment it was true. "They'll realize that, too, when they can think again. But meanwhile, you'd better get out."

"Get out . . . yes," said Stefan. The look of disorientation was gone, and there was a searing bitterness in the way he pronounced the words. "I will . . . get out."

"Stefan . . ."

"Matt." The green eyes were dark and burning, and Matt found he could not look away from them. "Is Elena safe? Good. Then, take care of her. Please."

"Stefan, what are you talking about? You're innocent; this will all blow over. . . ."

"Just take care of her, Matt."

Matt stepped back, still looking into those compelling green eyes. Then, slowly, he nodded.

"I will," he said quietly. And watched Stefan go.

Thirteen

Elena stood within the circle of adults and police, waiting for a chance to escape. She knew that Matt had warned Stefan in time—his face told her that—but he hadn't been able to get close enough to speak with her.

At last, with all attention turned toward the body, she detached herself from the group and edged toward Matt.

"Stefan got out all right," he said, his eyes on the group of adults. "But he told me to take care of you, and I want you to stay here."

"To take *care* of me?" Alarm and suspicion flashed through Elena. Then, almost in a whisper, she said, "I see." She thought a moment and then spoke carefully. "Matt, I need to go wash my hands. Bonnie got blood on me. Wait here; I'll be back."

He started to say something in protest, but she was already moving away. She held up her stained hands in explanation as she reached the door of the girls' locker room, and the teacher who was now standing there let her through. Once in the locker room, however, she kept on going, right out the far door and into the darkened school. And from there, into the night.

Zuccone! Stefan thought, grabbing a bookcase and flinging it over, sending its contents flying. Fool! Blind, hateful fool. How could he have been so stupid?

Find a place with them here? Be accepted as one of them? He must have been mad to have thought it was possible.

He picked up one of the great heavy trunks and threw it across the room, where it crashed against the far wall, splintering a window. Stupid, *stupid.*

Who was after him? Everybody. Matt had said it. *"There's been another attack. . . . They think you did it."*

Well, for once it looked as if the *barbari,* the petty living humans with their fear of anything unknown, were right. How else did you explain what had happened? He had felt the weakness, the spinning, swirling confusion; and then dark-

221

ness had taken him. When he'd awakened it was to hear Matt saying that another human had been pillaged, assaulted. Robbed this time not only of his blood, but of his life. How did you explain *that* unless he, Stefan, were the killer?

A killer was what he was. Evil. A creature born in the dark, destined to live and hunt and hide there forever. Well, why not kill, then? Why not fulfill his nature? Since he could not change it, he might as well revel in it. He would unleash his darkness upon this town that hated him, that hunted him even now.

But first . . . he was thirsty. His veins burned like a network of dry, hot wires. He needed to feed . . . soon . . . now.

The boarding house was dark. Elena knocked at the door but received no answer. Thunder cracked overhead. There was still no rain.

After the third barrage of knocking, she tried the door, and it opened. Inside, the house was silent and pitch black. She made her way to the staircase by feel and went up it.

The second landing was just as dark, and she stumbled, trying to find the bedroom with the stairway to the third floor. A faint light showed at the top of the stairs, and she climbed toward it, feeling oppressed by the walls, which seemed to close in on her from either side.

The light came from beneath the closed door. Elena tapped on it lightly and quickly. "Stefan," she whispered, and then she called more loudly, "Stefan, it's me."

No answer. She grasped the knob and pushed the door open, peering around the side. "Stefan—"

She was speaking to an empty room.

And a room filled with chaos. It looked as if some great wind had torn through, leaving destruction in its path. The trunks that had stood in corners so sedately were lying at grotesque angles, their lids gaping open, their contents strewn about the floor. One window was shattered. All Stefan's possessions, all the things he had kept so carefully and seemed to prize, were scattered like rubbish.

Terror swept through Elena. The fury, the violence in this scene of devastation were painfully clear, and they made her feel almost giddy. Somebody who has a history of violence, Tyler had said.

I don't care, she thought, anger surging up to push back the fear. I don't care about anything, Stefan; I still want to see you. But where are you?

The trapdoor in the ceiling was open, and cold air was blowing down. Oh, thought Elena, and she had a sudden chill of fear. That roof was so high. . . .

She'd never climbed the ladder to the widow's walk before, and her long skirt made it difficult. She emerged through the trapdoor slowly, kneeling on the roof and then standing up. She saw a dark figure in the corner, and she moved toward it quickly.

"Stefan, I had to come—" she began, and broke off short, because a flash of lightning lit the sky just as the figure in the corner whirled around. And then it was as if every foreboding and fear and nightmare she'd ever had were coming true all at once. It was beyond screaming at; it was beyond anything.

Oh, God . . . no. Her mind refused to make sense of what her eyes were seeing. No. No. She wouldn't look at this, she wouldn't believe it. . . .

But she could not help seeing. Even if she could have shut her eyes, every detail of the scene was etched upon her memory. As if the flash of lightning had seared it onto her brain forever.

Stefan. Stefan, so sleek and elegant in his ordinary clothes, in his black leather jacket with the collar turned up. Stefan, with his dark hair like one of the roiling storm clouds behind him. Stefan had been caught in that flash of light, half turned toward her, his body twisted into a bestial crouch, with a snarl of animal fury on his face.

And blood. That arrogant, sensitive, sensual mouth was smeared with blood. It showed ghastly red against the pallor of his skin, against the sharp whiteness of his bared teeth. In his hands was the limp body of a mourning dove, white as those teeth, wings outspread. Another lay on the ground at his feet, like a crumpled and discarded handkerchief.

"Oh, God, no," Elena whispered. She went on whispering it, backing away, scarcely aware that she was doing either. Her mind simply could not cope with this horror; her thoughts were running wildly in panic, like mice trying to escape a cage. She wouldn't believe this, she wouldn't *believe.* Her body was filled with unbearable tension, her heart was bursting, her head reeling.

"Oh, God, *no*—"

"Elena!" More terrible than anything else was this, to see *Stefan* looking at her out of that animal face, to see the snarl changing into a look of shock and desperation. "Elena, please. Please, don't . . ."

"Oh, God, *no!*" The screams were trying to rip their way out of her throat. She backed farther away, stumbling, as he took a step toward her. "No!"

"Elena, please—be careful—" That terrible thing, the thing with Stefan's face, was coming after her, green eyes burning. She flung herself backward as he took another step, his hand outstretched. That long, slender-fingered hand that had stroked her hair so gently—

"Don't *touch* me!" she cried. And then she did scream, as her motion brought her back against the iron railing of the widow's walk. It was iron that had been there for nearly a century and a half, and in places it was nearly rusted through. Elena's panicked weight against it was too much, and she felt it give way. She heard the tearing sound of overstressed metal and wood mingling with her own shriek. And then there was nothing behind her, nothing to grab on to, and she was falling.

In that instant, she saw the seething purple clouds, the dark bulk of the house beside her. It seemed that she had enough time to see them clearly, and to feel an infinity of terror as she screamed and fell, and fell.

But the terrible, shattering impact never came. Suddenly there were arms around her, supporting her in the void. There was a dull thud and the arms tightened, weight giving against her, absorbing the crash. Then all was still.

She held herself motionless within the circle of those arms, trying to get her bearings. Trying to believe yet another unbelievable thing. She had fallen from a three-story roof, and yet she was alive. She was standing in the garden behind the boarding house, in the utter silence between claps of thunder, with fallen leaves on the ground where her broken body should be.

Slowly, she brought her gaze upward to the face of the one who held her. Stefan.

There had been too much fear, too many blows tonight. She could react no longer. She could only stare up at him with a kind of wonder.

There was such sadness in his eyes. Those eyes that had burned like green ice were now dark and empty, hopeless. The same look that she'd seen that first night in his room, only now it was worse. For now there was self-hatred mixed with the sorrow, and bitter condemnation. She couldn't bear it.

"Stefan," she whispered, feeling that sadness

enter her own soul. She could still see the tinge of red on his lips, but now it awakened a thrill of pity along with the instinctive horror. To be so alone, so alien and so alone . . .

"Oh, Stefan," she whispered.

There was no answer in those bleak, lost eyes. "Come," he said quietly, and led her back toward the house.

Stefan felt a rush of shame as they reached the third story and the destruction that was his room. That Elena, of all people, should see this was insupportable. But then, perhaps it was also fitting that she should see what he truly was, what he could do.

She moved slowly, dazedly to the bed and sat. Then she looked up at him, her shadowed eyes meeting his. "Tell me," was all she said.

He laughed shortly, without humor, and saw her flinch. It made him hate himself more. "What do you need to know?" he said. He put a foot on the lid of an overturned trunk and faced her almost defiantly, indicating the room with a gesture. "Who did this? I did."

"You're strong," she said, her eyes on a capsized trunk. Her gaze lifted upward, as if she were remembering what had happened on the roof. "And quick."

"Stronger than a human," he said, with deliberate emphasis on the last word. Why didn't she cringe from him now, why didn't she look at him with the loathing he had seen before? He didn't care what she thought any longer. "My reflexes are faster, and I'm more resilient. I have to be. I'm a hunter," he said harshly.

Something in her look made him remember how she had interrupted him. He wiped his mouth with the back of his hand, then went quickly to pick up a glass of water that stood unharmed on the nightstand. He could feel her eyes on him as he drank it and wiped his mouth again. Oh, he still cared what she thought, all right.

"You can eat and drink . . . other things," she said.

"I don't need to," he said quietly, feeling weary and subdued. "I don't need anything else." He whipped around suddenly and felt passionate intensity rise in him again. "You said I was quick—but that's just what I'm not. Have you ever heard the saying 'the quick and the dead,' Elena? Quick means living; it means those who have life. I'm the other half."

He could see that she was trembling. But her voice was calm, and her eyes never left his. "Tell

229

me," she said again. "Stefan, I have a right to know."

He recognized those words. And they were as true as when she had first said them. "Yes, I suppose you do," he said, and his voice was tired and hard. He stared at the broken window for a few heartbeats and then looked back at her and spoke flatly. "I was born in the late fifteenth century. Do you believe that?"

She looked at the objects that lay where he'd scattered them from the bureau with one furious sweep of his arm. The florins, the agate cup, his dagger. "Yes," she said softly. "Yes, I believe it."

"And you want to know more? How I came to be what I am?" When she nodded, he turned to the window again. How could he tell her? He, who had avoided questions for so long, who had become such an expert at hiding and deceiving.

There was only one way, and that was to tell the absolute truth, concealing nothing. To lay it all before her, what he had never offered to any other soul.

And he wanted to do it. Even though he knew it would make her turn away from him in the end, he needed to show Elena what he was.

And so, staring into the darkness outside the

window, where flashes of blue brilliance occasionally lit the sky, he began.

He spoke dispassionately, without emotion, carefully choosing his words. He told her of his father, that solid Renaissance man, and of his world in Florence and at their country estate. He told her of his studies and his ambitions. Of his brother, who was so different than he, and of the ill feeling between them.

"I don't know when Damon started hating me," he said. "It was always that way, as long as I can remember. Maybe it was because my mother never really recovered from my birth. She died a few years later. Damon loved her very much, and I always had the feeling that he blamed me." He paused and swallowed. "And then, later, there was a girl."

"The one I remind you of?" Elena said softly. He nodded. "The one," she said, more hesitantly, "who gave you the ring?"

He glanced down at the silver ring on his finger, then met her eyes. Then, slowly, he drew out the ring he wore on the chain beneath his shirt and looked at it.

"Yes. This was her ring," he said. "Without such a talisman, we die in sunlight as if in a fire."

"Then she was . . . like you?"

"She made me what I am." Haltingly, he told her about Katherine. About Katherine's beauty and sweetness, and about his love for her. And about Damon's.

"She was too gentle, filled with too much affection," he said at last, painfully. "She gave it to everyone, including my brother. But finally, we told her she had to choose between us. And then . . . she came to me."

The memory of that night, of that sweet, terrible night came sweeping back. She had come to him. And he had been so happy, so full of awe and joy. He tried to tell Elena about that, to find the words. All that night he had been so happy, and even the next morning, when he had awakened and she was gone, he had been throned on highest bliss. . . .

It might almost have been a dream, but the two little wounds on his neck were real. He was surprised to find that they did not hurt and that they seemed to be partially healed already. They were hidden by the high neck of his shirt.

Her blood burned in his veins now, he thought, and the very words made his heart race. She had given her strength to him; she had chosen him.

He even had a smile for Damon when they

met at the designated place that evening. Damon had been absent from the house all day, but he showed up in the meticulously land-scaped garden precisely on time, and stood lounging against a tree, adjusting his cuff. Katherine was late.

"Perhaps she is tired," Stefan suggested, watching the melon-colored sky fade into deep midnight blue. He tried to keep the shy smug-ness from his voice. "Perhaps she needs more rest than usual."

Damon glanced at him sharply, his dark eyes piercing under the shock of black hair. "Per-haps," he said on a rising note, as if he would have said more.

But then they heard a light step on the path, and Katherine appeared between the box hedges. She was wearing her white gown, and she was as beautiful as an angel.

She had a smile for both of them. Stefan re-turned the smile politely, speaking their secret only with his eyes. Then he waited.

"You asked me to make my choice," she said, looking first at him and then at his brother. "And now you have come at the hour I ap-pointed, and I will tell you what I have chosen."

She held up her small hand, the one with the ring on it, and Stefan looked at the stone, realizing it was the same deep blue as the evening sky. It was as if Katherine carried a piece of the night with her, always.

"You have both seen this ring," she said quietly. "And you know that without it I would die. It is not easy to have such talismans made, but fortunately my woman Gudren is clever. And there are many silversmiths in Florence."

Stefan was listening without comprehension, but when she turned to him he smiled again, encouragingly.

"And so," she said, gazing into his eyes. "I have had a present made for you." She took his hand and pressed something into it. When he looked he saw that it was a ring in the same fashion as her own, but larger and heavier, and wrought in silver instead of gold.

"You do not need it yet to face the sun," she said softly, smiling. "But very soon you will."

Pride and rapture made him mute. He reached for her hand to kiss it, wanting to take her into his arms right then, even in front of Damon. But Katherine was turning away.

"And for you," she said, and Stefan thought his ears must be betraying him, for surely the warmth, the fondness in Katherine's voice could not be for his brother, "for you, also. You will need it very soon as well."

Stefan's eyes must be traitors, too. They were showing him what was impossible, what could not be. Into Damon's hand Katherine was putting a ring just like his own.

The silence that followed was absolute, like the silence after the world's ending.

"Katherine—" Stefan could barely force out the words. "How can you give that to *him?* After what we shared—"

"What *you* shared?" Damon's voice was like the crack of a whip, and he turned on Stefan angrily. "Last night she came to *me.* The choice is already made." And Damon jerked down his high collar to show two tiny wounds in his throat. Stefan stared at them, fighting down the bright sickness. They were identical to his own wounds.

He shook his head in utter bewilderment. "But, Katherine . . . it was not a dream. You came to *me* . . ."

"I came to both of you." Katherine's voice was tranquil, even pleased, and her eyes were serene. She smiled at Damon and then at Stefan in turn. "It has weakened me, but I am so glad I did. Don't you see?" she continued as they stared at her, too stunned to speak. "This is my choice! I love you both, and I will not give either of you up. Now we all three will be together, and be happy."

"Happy—" Stefan choked out.

"Yes, happy! The three of us will be companions, joyous companions, forever." Her voice rose with elation, and the light of a radiant child shone in her eyes. "We will be together always, never feeling sickness, never growing old, until the end of time! That is my choice."

"Happy . . . with *him?*" Damon's voice was shaking with fury, and Stefan saw that his normally self-contained brother was white with rage. "With this *boy* standing between us, this prating, mouthing paragon of virtue? I can barely stand the sight of him now. I wish to God that I should never see him again, never hear his voice again!"

"And I wish the same of *you,* brother," snarled Stefan, his heart tearing in his breast. This was Damon's fault; Damon had poisoned Katherine's mind so that she no longer knew what she was doing. "And I have half a mind to make sure of it," he added savagely.

Damon did not mistake his meaning. "Then get your sword, if you can find it," he hissed back, his eyes black with menace.

"Damon, Stefan, please! Please, no!" Katherine cried, putting herself between them, catching Stefan's arm. She looked from one to the other, her blue eyes wide with shock and bright with unshed tears. "Think of what you are saying. You are brothers."

"By no fault of mine," Damon grated, making the words a curse.

"But can you not make peace? For me, Damon . . . Stefan? *Please.*"

Part of Stefan wanted to melt at Katherine's desperate look, at her tears. But wounded pride and jealousy were too strong, and he knew his face was as hard, as unyielding, as Damon's.

"No," he said. "We cannot. It must be one or the other, Katherine. I will never share you with *him.*"

Katherine's hand fell away from his arm, and the tears fell from her eyes, great droplets that splashed onto the white gown. She caught her breath in a wrenching sob. Then, still weeping, she picked up her skirts and ran.

"And then Damon took the ring she had given him and put it on," Stefan said, his voice hoarse with use and emotion. "And he said to me, 'I'll have her yet, *brother.*' And then he walked away." He turned, blinking as if he'd come into a bright light from the dark, and looked at Elena.

She was sitting quite still on the bed, watching him with those eyes that were so much like Katherine's. Especially now, when they were filled with sorrow and dread. But Elena did not run. She spoke to him.

"And . . . what happened then?"

Stefan's hands clenched violently, reflexively, and he jerked away from the window. Not that memory. He could not endure that memory himself, much less try to *speak* it. How could he do that? How could he take Elena down into that darkness and show her the terrible things lurking there?

"No," he said. "I can't. I *can't.*"

"You have to tell me," she said softly. "Stefan, it's the end of the story, isn't it? That's what's behind all your walls, that's what you're afraid to let me see. But you must let me see it. Oh, Stefan, you can't stop now."

He could feel the horror reaching for him, the yawning pit he had seen so clearly, felt so clearly that day long ago. The day when it had all ended—when it had all begun.

He felt his hand taken, and when he looked he saw Elena's fingers closed about it, giving him warmth, giving him strength. Her eyes were on his. "Tell me."

"You want to know what happened next,

what became of Katherine?" he whispered. She nodded, her eyes nearly blind but still steady. "I'll tell you, then. She died the next day. My brother Damon and I, we killed her."

Fourteen

Elena felt her flesh creep at the words.

"You don't mean that," she said shakily. She remembered what she had seen on the roof, the blood smeared on Stefan's lips, and she forced herself not to recoil from him. "Stefan, I know you. You couldn't have done that. . . ."

He ignored her protestations, just went on staring with eyes that burned like the green ice at the bottom of a glacier. He was looking through her, into some incomprehensible distance. "As I lay in bed that night, I hoped against hope that she would come. Already I was noticing some of the changes in myself. I could see better in the dark; it seemed I could hear better. I felt stronger than ever before, full of some elemental energy. And I was hungry.

"It was a hunger I had never imagined. At

dinner I found that ordinary food and drink did nothing to satisfy it. I couldn't understand that. And then I saw the white neck of one of the serving girls, and I knew why." He drew a long breath, his eyes dark and tortured. "That night, I resisted the need, though it took all my will. I was thinking of Katherine, and praying she would come to me. Praying!" He gave a short laugh. "If a creature like me can pray."

Elena's fingers were numb within his grasp, but she tried to tighten them, to send him reassurance. "Go on, Stefan."

He had no trouble speaking now. He seemed almost to have forgotten her presence, as if he were telling this story to himself.

"The next morning the need was stronger. It was as if my own veins were dry and cracked, desperate for moisture. I knew that I couldn't stand it for long.

"I went to Katherine's chambers. I meant to ask her, to plead with her —" His voice cracked. He paused and then went on. "But Damon was there already, waiting outside her rooms. I could see that *he* hadn't resisted the need. The glow of his skin, the spring in his step, told me that. He looked as smug as the cat who's had the cream.

"But he hadn't had Katherine. 'Knock all you like,' he said to me, 'but the female dragon inside won't let you past. I've tried already. Shall we overpower her, you and I?'

"I wouldn't answer him. The look on his face, that sly, self-satisfied look, repelled me. I pounded on that door to wake . . ." He faltered, and then gave another humorless laugh. "I was going to say, 'to wake the dead.' But the dead aren't so hard to wake after all, are they?" After a moment, he went on.

"The maid, Gudren, opened the door. She had a face like a flat white plate, and eyes like black glass. I asked her if I could see her mistress. I expected to be told that Katherine was asleep, but instead Gudren just looked at me, then at Damon over my shoulder.

" 'I would not tell *him,*' she said at last, 'but I will tell you. My lady Katerina is not within. She went out early this morning, to walk in the gardens. She said she had much need of thought.'

"I was surprised. 'Early this morning?' I said.

" 'Yes,' she replied. She looked at both Damon and me without liking. 'My mistress was very unhappy last night,' she said meaningfully. 'All night long, she wept.'

"When she said that, a strange feeling came over me. It wasn't just shame and grief that Katherine should be so unhappy. It was fear. I forgot my hunger and weakness. I even forgot my enmity for Damon. I was filled with haste and a great driving urgency. I turned to Damon and told him that we had to find Katherine, and to my surprise he just nodded.

"We began to search the gardens, calling Katherine's name. I remember just what everything looked like that day. The sun was shining on the high cypress trees and the pines in the garden. Damon and I hurried between them, moving more and more quickly, and calling. We kept calling her . . ."

Elena could feel the tremors in Stefan's body, communicated to her through his tightly gripping fingers. He was breathing rapidly but shallowly.

"We had almost reached the end of the gardens when I remembered a place that Katherine had loved. It was a little way out onto the grounds, a low wall beside a lemon tree. I started there, shouting for her. But as I got closer, I stopped shouting. I felt . . . a fear—a terrible premonition. And I knew I mustn't—mustn't go—"

"Stefan!" said Elena. He was hurting her, his fingers biting into her own, crushing them. The tremors racing through his body were growing, becoming shudders. "Stefan, please!"

But he gave no sign that he heard her. "It was

like—a nightmare—everything happening so slowly. I couldn't move—and yet I had to. I had to keep walking. With each step, the fear grew stronger. I could smell it. A smell like burned fat. I mustn't go there—I don't want to see it—"

His voice had become high and urgent, his breath coming in gasps. His eyes were wide and dilated, like a terrified child's. Elena gripped his viselike fingers with her other hand, enfolding them completely. "Stefan, it's all right. You're not there. You're here with me."

"I don't want to see it—but I can't help it. There's something white. Something white under the tree. Don't make me look at it!"

"Stefan, Stefan, look at me!"

He was beyond hearing. His words came in heaving spasms, as if he could not control them, could not get them out fast enough. "I can't go any closer—but I do. I see the tree, the wall. And that white. Behind the tree. White with gold underneath. And then I know, I know, and I'm moving toward it because it's her dress. Katherine's white dress. And I get around the tree and I see it on the ground and it's true. It's Katherine's dress"—his voice rose and broke in unimaginable horror—"but Katherine isn't in it."

Elena felt a chill, as if her body had been

plunged into ice water. Her skin rose in goose-flesh, and she tried to speak to him but couldn't. He was rattling on as if he could keep the terror away if he kept on talking.

"Katherine isn't there, so maybe it's all a joke, but her dress is on the ground and it's full of ashes. Like the ashes in the hearth, just like that, only these smell of burned flesh. They stink. The smell is making me sick and faint. Beside the sleeve of the dress is a piece of parchment. And on a rock, on a rock a little way away is a ring. A ring with a blue stone, Katherine's ring. Katherine's ring . . ." Suddenly, he called out in a terrible voice, "Katherine, what have you *done?*" Then he fell to his knees, releasing Elena's fingers at last, to bury his face in his hands.

Elena held him as he was gripped by wracking sobs. She held his shoulders, pulling him to her lap. "Katherine took the ring off," she whispered. It was not a question. "She exposed herself to the sun."

His harsh sobs went on and on, as she held him to the full skirts of the blue gown, stroking his quivering shoulders. She murmured nonsense meant to soothe him, pushing away her own horror. And, presently, he quieted and lifted his head. He spoke thickly, but he seemed to have returned to the present, to have come back.

"The parchment was a note, for me and for Damon. It said she had been selfish, wanting to have both of us. It said—she couldn't bear to be the cause of strife between us. She hoped that once she was gone we would no longer hate each other. She did it to bring us together."

"Oh, Stefan," whispered Elena. She felt burning tears fill her own eyes in sympathy. "Oh, Stefan, I'm so sorry. But don't you see, after all this time, that what Katherine did was wrong? It was selfish, even, and it was *her* choice. In a way, it had nothing to do with you, or with Damon."

Stefan shook his head as if to shake off the truth of the words. "She gave her life . . . for that. We killed her." He was sitting up now. But his eyes were still dilated, great disks of black, and he had the look of a small bewildered boy.

"Damon came up behind me. He took the note and read it. And then—I think he went mad. We were both mad. I had picked up Katherine's ring, and he tried to take it. He shouldn't have. We struggled. We said terrible things to each other. We each blamed the other for what had happened. I don't remember how we got back to the house, but suddenly I had my sword. We were fighting. I wanted to destroy that arrogant face forever, to kill him. I remember my father shouting from the house. We fought harder, to finish it before he reached us.

"And we were well matched. But Damon had always been stronger, and that day he seemed faster, too, as if he had changed more than I had. And so while my father was still shouting from the window I felt Damon's blade get past my guard. Then I felt it enter my heart."

Elena stared, aghast, but he went on without pause. "I felt the pain of the steel, I felt it stab through me, deep, deep inside. All the way through, a hard thrust. And then the strength poured out of me and I fell. I lay there on the paved ground."

He looked up at Elena and finished simply, "And that is how . . . I died."

Elena sat frozen, as if the ice she'd felt in her chest earlier tonight had flooded out and trapped her.

"Damon came and stood over me and bent down. I could hear my father's cries from far away, and screams from the household, but all I could see was Damon's face. Those black eyes that were like a moonless night. I wanted to hurt him for what he had done to me. For everything he had done to me, and to Katherine." Stefan was quiet a moment, and then he said, almost dreamily, "And so I lifted my sword and I killed him. With the last of my strength, I stabbed my brother through the heart."

The storm had moved on, and through the broken window Elena could hear soft night noises, the chirp of crickets, the wind sifting through trees. In Stefan's room, it was very still.

"I knew nothing more until I woke up in my tomb," said Stefan. He leaned back, away from her, and shut his eyes. His face was pinched and weary, but that awful childlike dreaminess was gone.

"Both Damon and I had had just enough of Katherine's blood to keep us from truly dying. Instead we changed. We woke together in our tomb, dressed in our best clothing, laid on slabs side by side. We were too weak to hurt each other anymore; the blood had been just barely enough. And we were confused. I called to Damon, but he ran outside into the night.

"Fortunately, we had been buried with the rings Katherine had given us. And I found her ring in my pocket." As if unconsciously, Stefan reached up to stroke the golden circlet. "I suppose they thought she had given it to me.

"I tried to go home. That was stupid. The servants screamed at the sight of me and ran to fetch a priest. I ran, too. Into the only place where I was safe, into the dark.

"And that is where I've stayed ever since. It's where I belong, Elena. I killed Katherine with my pride and my jealousy, and I killed Damon with my hatred. But I did worse than kill my brother. I damned him.

"If he hadn't died then, with Katherine's blood so strong in his veins, he would have had a chance. In time the blood would have grown weaker, and then passed away. He would have become a normal human again. By killing him then, I condemned him to live in the night. I took away his only chance of salvation."

Stefan laughed bitterly. "Do you know what the name Salvatore means in Italian, Elena? It means salvation, savior. I'm named that, and for St. Stephen, the first Christian martyr. And I damned my brother to hell."

"No," said Elena. And then, in a stronger voice, she said, "No, Stefan. He damned himself. He killed *you*. But what happened to him after that?"

"For a while he joined one of the Free Companies, ruthless mercenaries whose business was to rob and plunder. He wandered across the country with them, fighting and drinking the blood of his victims.

"I was living beyond the city gates by then, half starved, preying on animals, an animal myself. For a long time, I heard nothing about Damon. Then one day I heard his voice in my mind.

"He was stronger than I, because he was drinking human blood. And killing. Humans have the strongest life essence, and their blood gives power. And when they're killed, somehow the life essence they give is strongest of all. It's as if in those last moments of terror and struggle the soul is the most vibrant. Because Damon killed humans, he was able to draw on the Powers more than I was."

"What . . . powers?" said Elena. A thought was growing in her mind.

"Strength, as you said, and quickness. A sharpening of all the senses, especially at night. Those are the basics. We can also . . . feel minds. We can sense their presence, and sometimes the nature of their thoughts. We can cast confusion about weaker minds, either to overwhelm them or to bend them to our will. There are others. With enough human blood we can change our shapes, become animals. And the more you kill, the stronger all the Powers become.

"Damon's voice in my mind was very strong.

He said he was now the *condottieri* of his own company and he was coming back to Florence. He said that if I was there when he arrived he would kill me. I believed him, and I left. I've seen him once or twice since then. The threat is always the same, and he's always more powerful. Damon's made the most of his nature, and he seems to glory in its darkest side.

"But it's my nature, too. The same darkness is inside me. I thought that I could conquer it, but I was wrong. That's why I came here, to Fell's Church. I thought if I settled in some small town, far away from the old memories, I might escape the darkness. And instead, tonight, I killed a man."

"No," said Elena forcefully. "I don't believe that, Stefan." His story had filled her with horror and pity . . . and fear, too. She admitted that. But her disgust had vanished, and there was one thing she was sure about. Stefan wasn't a murderer. "What happened tonight, Stefan? Did you argue with Tanner?"

"I . . . don't remember," he said bleakly. "I used the Power to persuade him to do what you wanted. Then I left. But later I felt the dizziness and the weakness come over me. As it has before." He looked up at her directly. "The last time it happened was in the cemetery, right by the church, the night Vickie Bennett was attacked."

"But you didn't do that. You *couldn't* have done that. . . . Stefan?"

"I don't know," he said harshly. "What other explanation is there? And I did take blood from the old man under the bridge, that night you girls ran away from the graveyard. I would have sworn I didn't take enough to harm him, but he almost died. And I was there when both Vickie and Tanner were attacked."

"But you don't remember attacking them," said Elena, relieved. The idea that had been growing in her mind was now almost a certainty.

"What difference does it make? Who else could have done it, if not me?"

"Damon," said Elena.

He flinched, and she saw his shoulders tighten again. "It's a nice thought. I hoped at first that there might be some explanation like that. That it might be someone else, someone like my brother. But I've searched with my mind and found nothing, no other presence. The simplest explanation is that I'm the killer."

"No," said Elena, "you don't understand. I don't just mean that someone like Damon might do the things we've seen. I mean Damon is here, in Fell's Church. I've seen him."

Stefan just stared at her.

"It must be him," Elena said, taking a deep breath. "I've seen him twice now, maybe three times. Stefan, you just told me a long story, and now I've got one to tell you."

As quickly and simply as she could, she told him about what had happened in the gym, and at Bonnie's house. His lips tightened into a white line as she told him how Damon had tried to kiss her. Her cheeks grew hot as she remembered her own response, how she had almost given in to him. But she told Stefan everything.

About the crow, too, and all the other strange things that had happened since she had come home from France.

"And, Stefan, I think Damon was at the Haunted House tonight," she finished. "Just after you felt dizzy in the front room, someone passed me. He was dressed up like—like Death, in black robes and a hood, and I couldn't see his face. But something about the way he moved was familiar. It was him, Stefan. Damon was there."

"But that still wouldn't explain the other times. Vickie and the old man. I *did* take blood from the old man." Stefan's face was taut, as if he were almost afraid to hope.

"But you said yourself you didn't take enough

to harm him. Stefan, who knows what happened to that man after you left? Wouldn't it be the easiest thing in the world for Damon to attack him then? Especially if Damon's been spying on you all along, maybe in some other form . . ."

"Like a crow," murmured Stefan.

"Like a crow. And as for Vickie . . . Stefan, you said that you can cast confusion over weaker minds, overpower them. Couldn't that be what Damon was doing to you? Overpowering your mind as you can overpower a human's?"

"Yes, and shielding his presence from me." There was mounting excitement in Stefan's voice. "That's why he hasn't answered my calls. He wanted—"

"He wanted just what's happened to happen. He wanted you to doubt yourself, to think you were a killer. *But it isn't true, Stefan.* Oh, Stefan, you know that now, and you don't have to be afraid anymore." She stood up, feeling joy and relief course through her. Out of this hideous night, something wonderful had come.

"That's why you've been so distant with me, isn't it?" she said, holding out her hands to him. "Because you're afraid of what you might do. But there's no need for that any longer."

"Isn't there?" He was breathing quickly again, and he eyed her outstretched hands as if they were two snakes. "You think there's no reason to be afraid? Damon may have attacked those people, but he doesn't control my thoughts. And you don't know what I've thought about you."

Elena kept her voice level. "You don't want to hurt me," she said positively.

"No? There have been times, watching you in public, when I could scarcely bear not to touch you. When I was so tempted by your white throat, your little white throat with the faint blue veins beneath the skin . . ." His eyes were fixed on her neck in a way that reminded her of Damon's eyes, and she felt her heartbeat step up. "Times when I thought I would grab you and force you right there in the school."

"There's no need to force me," said Elena. She could feel her pulse everywhere now; in her wrists and the inside of her elbows—and in her throat. "I've made my decision, Stefan," she said softly, holding his eyes. "I want to."

He swallowed thickly. "You don't know what you're asking for."

"I think I do. You told me how it was with Katherine, Stefan. I want it to be like that with us. I don't mean I want you to change me. But we can share a little without that happening, can't we? I know," she added, even more softly, "how much you loved Katherine. But she's gone now, and I'm here. And I love you, Stefan. I want to be with you."

"You don't know what you're talking about!" He was standing rigid, his face furious, his eyes anguished. "If I once let go, what's to *keep* me from changing you, or killing you? The passion is stronger than you can imagine. Don't you understand yet what I am, what I can do?"

She stood there and looked at him quietly, her chin raised slightly. It seemed to enrage him.

"Haven't you seen enough yet? Or do I have to show you more? Can't you picture what I might do to you?" He strode over to the cold fireplace and snatched out a long piece of wood, thicker than both Elena's wrists together. With one motion, he snapped it in two like a match stick. "*Your* fragile bones," he said.

Across the room was a pillow from the bed; he caught it up and with a slash of his nails left the silk cover in ribbons. "*Your* soft skin." Then he moved toward Elena with preternatural quickness; he was there and had hold of her shoulders before she knew what was happening. He stared into her face a moment, then, with a savage hiss that raised the hairs at the nape of her neck, drew his lips back.

It was the same snarl she'd seen on the roof, those white teeth bared, the canines grown to unbelievable length and sharpness. They were the fangs of a predator, a hunter. *"Your* white neck," he said in a distorted voice.

Elena stood paralyzed another instant, gazing as if compelled into that chilling visage, and then something deep in her unconscious took over. She reached up within the restraining circle of his arms and caught his face between her two hands. His cheeks were cool against her palms. She held him that way, softly, so softly, as if to reprove his hard grip on her bare shoulders. And she saw the confusion slowly come to his face, as he realized she was not doing it to fight him or to shove him away.

Elena waited until that confusion reached his eyes, shattering his gaze, becoming almost a look of pleading. She knew that her own face was fearless, soft yet intense, her lips slightly parted. They were both breathing quickly now, together, in rhythm. Elena could feel it when he started to shake, trembling as he had when the memories of Katherine had become too much to bear. Then, very gently and deliberately, she drew that snarling mouth down to her own.

He tried to oppose her. But her gentleness was stronger than all his inhuman strength. She shut her eyes and thought only of Stefan, not of the dreadful things she had learned tonight but of Stefan, who had stroked her hair as lightly as if she might break in his hands. She thought of that, and she kissed the predatory mouth that had threatened her a few minutes ago.

She felt the change, the transformation in his mouth as he yielded, responding helplessly to her, meeting her soft kisses with equal softness. She felt the shudder go through Stefan's body as the hard grip on her shoulders softened, too, becoming an embrace. And she knew she'd won.

"You will never hurt me," she whispered.

It was as if they were kissing away all the fear and desolation and loneliness inside them. Elena felt passion surge through her like summer lightning, and she could sense the answering passion in Stefan. But infusing everything else was a gentleness almost frightening in its intensity. There was no need for haste or roughness, Elena thought as Stefan gently guided her to sit down.

Gradually, the kisses grew more urgent, and Elena felt the summer lightning flicker all through her body, charging it, making her heart pound and her breath catch. It made her feel strangely soft and dizzy, made her shut her eyes and let her head fall back in abandon.

It's time, Stefan, she thought. And, very gently, she drew his mouth down again, this time to her throat. She felt his lips graze her skin, felt his breath warm and cool at once. Then she felt the sharp sting.

But the pain faded almost instantly. It was replaced by a feeling of pleasure that made her tremble. A great rushing sweetness filled her, flowing through her to Stefan.

At last she found herself gazing into his face, into a face that at last had no barriers against her, no walls. And the look she saw there made her feel weak.

"Do you trust me?" he whispered. And when she simply nodded, he held her eyes and reached for something beside the bed. It was the dagger. She regarded it without fear, and then fixed her eyes again on his face.

He never looked away from her as he unsheathed it and made a small cut at the base of his throat. Elena looked at it wide-eyed, at the blood as bright as holly berries, but when he urged her forward she did not try to resist him.

Afterward he just held her a long time, while

the crickets outside made their music. Finally, he stirred.

"I wish you could stay here," he whispered. "I wish you could stay forever. But you can't."

"I know," she said, equally quiet. Their eyes met again in silent communion. There was so much to say, so many reasons to be together. "Tomorrow," she said. Then, leaning against his shoulder, she whispered, "Whatever happens, Stefan, I'll be with you. Tell me you believe that."

His voice was hushed, muffled in her hair. "Oh, Elena, I believe it. Whatever happens, we'll be together."

Fifteen

As soon as he left Elena at her house, Stefan went to the woods.

He took Old Creek Road, driving under the sullen clouds through which no patch of sky could be seen, to the place where he had parked on the first day of school.

Leaving the car, he tried to retrace his steps exactly to the clearing where he had seen the crow. His hunter's instincts helped him, recalling the shape of this bush and that knotted root, until he stood in the open place ringed with ancient oak trees.

Here. Under this blanket of dingy-brown leaves, some of the rabbit's bones might even remain.

Taking a long breath to still himself, to gather his Powers, he cast out a probing, demanding thought.

And for the first time since he'd come to Fell's Church, he felt the flicker of a reply. But it seemed faint and wavering, and he could not locate it in space.

He sighed and turned around—and stopped dead.

Damon stood before him, arms crossed over his chest, lounging against the largest oak tree. He looked as if he might have been there for hours.

"So," said Stefan heavily, "it is true. It's been a long time, brother."

"Not as long as you think, *brother.*" Stefan remembered that voice, that velvety, ironical voice. "I've kept track of you over the years," Damon said calmly. He flicked a bit of bark from the sleeve of his leather jacket as casually as he had once arranged his brocade cuffs. "But then, you wouldn't know that, would you? Ah, no, your Powers are as weak as ever."

"Be careful, Damon," Stefan said softly, dangerously. "Be very careful tonight. I'm not in a tolerant mood."

"St. Stefan in a pique? Imagine. You're distressed, I suppose, because of my little excursions into your territory. I only did it because I wanted to be close to you. Brothers should be close."

"You *killed* tonight. And you tried to make me think I'd done it."

"Are you quite sure you didn't? Perhaps we did it together. Careful!" he said as Stefan stepped toward him. "My mood is not the most tolerant tonight, either. I only had a wizened little history teacher; you had a pretty girl."

The fury inside Stefan coalesced, seeming to focus in one bright burning spot, like a sun inside him. "Keep away from Elena," he whispered with such menace that Damon actually tilted his head back slightly. "Keep away from her, Damon. I know you've been spying on her, watching her. But no more. Go near her again and you'll regret it."

"You always *were* selfish. Your one fault. Not willing to share anything, are you?" Suddenly, Damon's lips curved in a singularly beautiful smile. "But fortunately the lovely Elena is more generous. Didn't she tell you about our little liaisons? Why, the first time we met she almost gave herself to me on the spot."

"That's a lie!"

"Oh, no, dear brother. I never lie about anything important. Or do I mean unimportant? Anyway, your beauteous damsel nearly swooned into my arms. I think she likes men in black." As Stefan stared at him, trying to control his breathing, Damon added, almost gently, "You're wrong about her, you know. You think she's sweet and docile, like Katherine. She isn't. She's not your type at all, my saintly brother. She has a spirit and a fire in her that you wouldn't know what to do with."

"And you would, I suppose."

Damon uncrossed his arms and slowly smiled again. "Oh, yes."

Stefan wanted to leap for him, to smash that beautiful, arrogant smile, to tear Damon's throat out. He said, in a barely controlled voice, "You're right about one thing. She's strong. Strong enough to fight you off. And now that she knows what you really are, she will. All she feels for you now is disgust."

Damon's eyebrows lifted. "Does she, now? We'll see about that. Perhaps she'll find that real darkness is more to her taste than feeble twilight. I, at least, can admit the truth about my nature. But I worry about you, little brother. You're looking weak and ill-fed. She's a tease, is she?"

Kill him, something in Stefan's mind demanded. Kill him, snap his neck, rip his throat to bloody shreds. But he knew Damon had fed very well tonight. His brother's dark aura was swollen, pulsing, almost shining with the life essence he had taken.

"Yes, I drank deeply," Damon said pleasantly, as if he knew what was in Stefan's mind. He sighed and ran his tongue over his lips in satisfied remembrance. "He was small, but there was a surprising amount of juice in him. Not pretty like Elena, and he certainly didn't smell as good. But it's always exhilarating to feel the new blood singing inside you." Damon breathed expansively, stepping away from the tree and looking around. Stefan remembered those graceful movements, too, each gesture controlled and precise. The centuries had only refined Damon's natural poise.

"It makes me feel like doing this," said Damon, moving to a sapling a few yards away. It was half again as tall as he was, and when he grasped it his fingers did not meet around the trunk. But Stefan saw the quick breath and the ripple of muscles under Damon's thin black shirt, and then the tree tore loose from the ground, its roots dangling. Stefan could smell the pungent dampness of disturbed earth.

"I didn't like it there anyway," said Damon, and heaved it as far away as the still-entangled roots would allow. Then he smiled engagingly. "It also makes me feel like doing *this*."

There was a shimmer of motion, and then Damon was gone. Stefan looked around but could see no sign of him.

"Up here, brother." The voice came from overhead, and when Stefan looked up he saw Damon perching among the spreading branches of the oak tree. There was a rustle of tawny brown leaves, and he disappeared again.

"Back here, brother." Stefan spun at the tap on his shoulder, only to see nothing behind him. "Right here, brother." He spun again. "No, try here." Furious, Stefan whipped the other way, trying to catch hold of Damon. But his fingers grasped only air.

Here, Stefan. This time the voice was in his mind, and the Power of it shook him to the core. It took enormous strength to project thoughts that clearly. Slowly, he turned around once more, to see Damon back in his original position, leaning against the big oak tree.

But this time the humor in those dark eyes had faded. They were black and fathomless, and Damon's lips were set in a straight line.

What more proof do you need, Stefan? I'm as much stronger than you as you are stronger than these pitiful humans. I'm faster than you, too, and I have other Powers you've scarcely heard of. The Old Pow-

266

ers, Stefan. And I'm not afraid to use them. If you fight me, I'll use them against you.

"Is that what you came here for? To torture me?"

I've been merciful with you, brother. Many times you've been mine for the killing, but I've always spared your life. But this time is different. Damon stepped away from the tree again and spoke aloud. "I am warning you, Stefan, don't oppose me. It doesn't matter what I came here for. What I want now is Elena. And if you try to stop me from taking her, I will kill you."

"You can try," said Stefan. The hot pinpoint of fury inside him burned brighter than ever, pouring forth its brilliance like a whole galaxy of stars. He knew, somehow, that it threatened Damon's darkness.

"You think I can't do it? You never learn, do you, little brother?" Stefan had just enough time to note Damon's weary shake of the head when there was another blur of motion and he felt strong hands seize him. He was fighting instantly, violently, trying with all his strength to throw them off. But they were like hands of steel.

He lashed out savagely, trying to strike at the vulnerable area under Damon's jaw. It did no good; his arms were pinioned behind him, his body immobilized. He was as helpless as a bird under the claws of a lean and expert cat.

He went limp for an instant, making himself a deadweight, and then he suddenly surged with all his muscles, trying to break free, trying to get a blow in. The cruel hands only tightened on him, making his struggles useless. Pathetic.

You always were stubborn. Perhaps this will convince you. Stefan looked into his brother's face, pale as the frosted-glass windows at the boarding house, and at those black bottomless eyes. Then he felt fingers grasp his hair, jerk his head back, exposing his throat.

His struggles redoubled, became frantic. *Don't bother,* came the voice in his head, and then he felt the sharp rending pain of teeth. He felt the humiliation and helplessness of the hunter's victim, of the hunted, of the prey. And then the pain of blood being drawn out against his will.

He refused to give in to it, and the pain grew worse, a feeling as if his soul was tearing loose like the sapling. It stabbed through him like spears of fire, concentrating on the punctures in his flesh where Damon's teeth had sunk in. Agony flamed up his jaw and cheek and down his chest and shoulder. He felt a wave of vertigo and realized he was losing consciousness.

Then, abruptly, the hands released him and

he fell to the ground, onto a bed of damp and moldering oak leaves. Gasping for breath, he painfully got to his hands and knees.

"You see, little brother, I'm stronger than you. Strong enough to take you, take your blood and your life if I wish it. Leave Elena to me, or I will."

Stefan looked up. Damon was standing with head thrown back, legs slightly apart, like a conqueror putting his foot on the neck of the conquered. Those night-black eyes were hot with triumph, and Stefan's blood was on his lips.

Hatred filled Stefan, such hatred as he had never known before. It was as if all his earlier hatred of Damon had been a drop of water to this crashing, foaming ocean. Many times in the last long centuries he had regretted what he had done to his brother, when he'd wished with all his soul to change it. Now he only wanted to do it again.

"Elena is not yours," he ground out, getting to his feet, trying not to show what an effort it cost him. "And she never will be." Concentrating on each step, putting one foot in front of the other, he began walking away. His entire body hurt, and the shame he felt was even greater than the physical ache. There were bits of wet leaves and crumbs of earth adhering to his clothes, but he did not brush them off. He fought to keep moving, to hold out against the weakness that lapped at his limbs.

You never learn, brother.

Stefan did not look back or try to reply. He gritted his teeth and kept his legs moving. Another step. And another step. And another step.

If he could just sit down for a moment, rest . . .

Another step, and another step. The car couldn't be far now. Leaves crackled under his feet, and then he heard leaves crackle behind him.

He tried to turn quickly, but his reflexes were almost gone. And the sharp motion was too much for him. Darkness filled him, filled his body and his mind, and he was falling. He fell forever into the black of absolute night. And then, mercifully, he knew no more.

Sixteen

Elena hurried toward Robert E. Lee, feeling as if she'd been away from it for years. Last night seemed like something from her distant childhood, barely remembered. But she knew that today there would be its consequences to face.

Last night she'd had to face Aunt Judith. Her aunt had been terribly upset when neighbors had told her about the murder, and even more upset that no one seemed to know where Elena was. By the time Elena had arrived home at nearly two in the morning, she had been frantic with worry.

Elena hadn't been able to explain. She could only say that she'd been with Stefan, and that she knew he had been accused, and that she knew was innocent. All the rest, everything else that had happened, she had had to keep to herself. Even if Aunt Judith had believed it, she would never have understood.

And this morning Elena had slept in, and now she was late. The streets were deserted except for her, as she hurried on toward the school. Overhead, the sky was gray and a wind was rising. She desperately wanted to see Stefan. All night, while she'd been sleeping so heavily, she'd had nightmares about him.

One dream had been especially real. In it she saw Stefan's pale face and his angry, accusing eyes. He held up a book to her and said, "How could you, Elena? How could you?" Then he dropped the book at her feet and walked away. She called after him, pleading, but he went on walking until he disappeared in darkness. When she looked down at the book, she saw it was bound in dark blue velvet. Her diary.

A quiver of anger went through her as she thought again of how her diary had been stolen. But what did the dream mean? What was in her diary to make Stefan look like that?

She didn't know. All she knew was that she needed to see him, to hear his voice, to feel his arms around her. Being away from him was like being separated from her own flesh.

She ran up the steps of the high school into the nearly empty corridors. She headed toward the foreign-language wing, because she knew that Stefan's first class was Latin. If she could just see him for a moment, she would be all right.

But he wasn't in class. Through the little window in the door, she saw his empty seat. Matt was there, and the expression on his face made her feel more frightened than ever. He kept glancing at Stefan's desk with a look of sick apprehension.

Elena turned away from the door mechanically. Like an automaton, she climbed the stairs and walked to her trigonometry classroom. As she opened the door, she saw every face turn toward her, and she slipped hastily into the empty desk beside Meredith.

Ms. Halpern stopped the lesson for a moment and looked at her, then continued. When the teacher had turned back to the blackboard, Elena looked at Meredith.

Meredith reached over to take her hand. "Are you all right?" she whispered.

"I don't know," said Elena stupidly. She felt as if the very air around her was smothering her, as if there were a crushing weight all around her. Meredith's fingers felt dry and hot. "Meredith, do you know what's happened to Stefan?"

"You mean *you* don't know?" Meredith's dark

eyes widened, and Elena felt the weight grow even more crushing. It was like being deep, deep under water without a pressure suit.

"They haven't . . . arrested him, have they?" she said, forcing the words out.

"Elena, it's worse than that. He's disappeared. The police went to the boarding house early this morning and he wasn't there. They came to school, too, but he never showed up today. They said they'd found his car abandoned out by Old Creek Road. Elena, they think he's left, skipped town, because he's guilty."

"That's not true," said Elena through her teeth. She saw people turn around and look at her, but she was beyond caring. "He's innocent!"

"I know you think so, Elena, but why else would he leave?"

"He wouldn't. He didn't." Something was burning inside Elena, a fire of anger that pushed back at the crushing fear. She was breathing raggedly. "He would never have left of his own free will."

"You mean someone forced him? But who? Tyler wouldn't dare—"

"Forced him, or worse," Elena interrupted. The entire class was staring at them now, and

Ms. Halpern was opening her mouth. Elena stood up suddenly, looking at them without seeing. "God help him if he's hurt Stefan," she said. "God *help* him." Then she whirled and made for the door.

"Elena, come back! Elena!" She could hear shouts behind her, Meredith's and Ms. Halpern's. She walked on, faster and faster, seeing only what was straight ahead of her, her mind fixed on one thing.

They thought she was going after Tyler Smallwood. Good. They could waste their time running in the wrong direction. She knew what she had to do.

She left the school, plunging into the cold autumn air. She moved quickly, legs eating up the distance between the school and the Old Creek Road. From there she turned toward Wickery Bridge and the graveyard.

An icy wind whipped her hair back and stung her face. Oak leaves were flying around her, swirling in the air. But the conflagration in her heart was searing hot and burned away the cold. She knew now what a towering rage meant. She strode past the purple beeches and the weeping willows into the center of the old graveyard and looked around her with feverish eyes.

Above, the clouds were flowing along like a

lead-gray river. The limbs of the oaks and beeches lashed together wildly. A gust threw handfuls of leaves into her face. It was as if the graveyard were trying to drive her out, as if it were showing her its power, gathering itself to do something awful to her.

Elena ignored all of it. She spun around, her burning gaze searching between the headstones. Then she turned and shouted directly into the fury of the wind. Just one word, but the one she knew would bring him.

"Damon!"

Don't miss the exciting continuation of
The Vampire Diaries

Volume II: THE STRUGGLE

One

"Damon!"

Icy wind whipped Elena's hair around her face, tearing at her light sweater. Oak leaves swirled among the rows of granite headstones, and the trees lashed their branches together in a frenzy. Elena's hands were cold, her lips and cheeks numb, but she stood facing the screaming wind directly, shouting into it.

"Damon!"

This weather was a show of his power, meant to frighten her away. It wouldn't work. The thought of that same power being turned against Stefan woke a hot fury inside her that burned against the wind. If Damon had done anything to Stefan, if Damon had hurt him . . .

"Damn you, answer me!" she shouted at the oak trees that bordered the graveyard.

A dead leaf like a withered brown hand skittered up to her foot, but there was no answer. Above, the sky was gray as glass, gray as the tombstones which surrounded her. Elena felt rage and frustration sting her throat and she sagged. She'd been wrong. Damon wasn't here after all; she was alone with the screaming wind.

She turned and gasped.

He was just behind her, so close that her clothes brushed his as she turned. At that distance, she should have sensed another human being standing there, should have felt his body-warmth or heard him. But of course Damon wasn't human.

She reeled back a couple of steps before she could stop herself. Every instinct that had lain quiet while she shouted into the violence of the wind was now begging her to run.

She clenched her fists. "Where's Stefan?"

A line appeared between Damon's dark eyebrows. "Stefan who?"

Elena stepped forward and slapped him.

She had no thought of doing it before she did it, and afterward she could scarcely believe what she had done. But it was a good hard slap, with the full force of her body behind it, and it snapped Damon's head to one side. Her hand stung. She stood, trying to calm her breath, and watched him.

He was dressed as she had first seen him, in black. Soft black boots, black jeans, black sweater, and leather jacket. And he looked like Stefan. She didn't know how she could have missed that before. He had the same dark hair, the same pale skin, the same disturbing good looks. But his hair was straight, not wavy, and his eyes were black as midnight, and his mouth was cruel.

He turned his head slowly back to look at her and she saw blood rising in the cheek she'd slapped.

"Don't lie to me," she said, her voice shaking. "I know who you are. I know *what* you are. You killed Mr. Tanner last night. And now Stefan's disappeared."

"Has he?"

"You know he has!"

Damon smiled, and then turned it off instantly.

"I'm warning you; if you've hurt him—"

"Then, what?" he said. "What will you do, Elena? What *can* you do, against me?"

Elena fell silent. For the first time she realized that the wind had died away. The day had gone deadly quiet around them, as if they stood motionless at the center of some great circle of power. It seemed as if everything, the leaden sky, the oaks and purple beeches, the ground itself, was connected to him, as if he drew power from all of it. He stood with his head tilted back slightly, his eyes fathomless and full of strange lights.

"I don't know," she whispered, "but I'll find something. Believe me."

He laughed suddenly and Elena's heart jerked and began pounding hard. God, he was beautiful. Handsome was too weak and colorless a word. As usual, the laughter lasted only a moment, but even when his lips had sobered it left traces in his eyes.

"I do believe you," he said, relaxing, looking around the graveyard. Then he turned back and held out a hand to her. "You're too good for my brother," he said casually.

Elena thought of slapping the hand away, but she didn't want to touch him again. "Tell me where he is."

"Later, possibly—for a price." He withdrew his hand.

"My brother," he went on, "is a fool. He thinks that because you look like Katherine you're weak and easily led like her. But he's wrong. I could feel your anger from the other side of town. I can feel it now, a white light like the desert sun. You're strong, Elena, even as you are. But you could be so much stronger . . ."

She stared at him, not understanding, not liking the change of subject. "I don't know what you're talking about. And what has it got to do with Stefan?"

"I'm talking about power, Elena." Suddenly, he stepped close to her, his eyes fixed on hers, his voice soft and urgent. "You've tried everything else, and nothing has satisfied you. You're the girl who has everything, but there's always been something just out of your reach, something you need desperately and can't have. That's what I'm offering you. Power. Eternal life. And feelings you've never felt before."

She *did* understand, then, and bile rose in her throat. She choked on horror and repudiation. "No."

"Why not?" he whispered. "Why not try it, Elena? Be honest, isn't there a part of you that wants to?" His dark eyes were full of a heat and intensity that held her transfixed, unable to look away. "I can waken things inside you that have been sleeping all your life. You're strong enough to live in the dark, to glory in it. You can become a queen of the shadows. Why not take that power, Elena? Let me help you take it."

"No," she said, wrenching her eyes away from his. She wouldn't look at him, wouldn't let him do this to her. She wouldn't let him make her forget . . . make her forget . . .

"It's the ultimate drug, Elena," he said. His voice was as caressing as the fingertips which touched her throat. "The ultimate secret. You'll be happy as never before."

There was something terribly important she must remember. He was using Power to make her forget it, but she wouldn't let him make her forget . . .

"And we'll be together, you and I." The cool fingertips stroked the side of her neck, slipping under the collar of her sweater. "Just the two of us, forever."

There was a sudden twinge of pain as his fingers brushed two tiny wounds in the flesh of her neck there, and her mind cleared.

Make her forget . . . *Stefan.*

That was what he wanted to drive out of her

mind. The memory of Stefan, of his green eyes and his smile that always had sadness lurking behind it. But nothing could force Stefan out of her thoughts now, not after what they had shared. She pulled away from Damon, knocking those cool fingertips aside. She looked straight at him.

"I've already found what I want," she said brutally. "And who I want to be with forever."

Blackness welled up in his eyes, a cold rage that swept through the air between them. Looking into those eyes, Elena thought of a cobra about to strike.

"Don't you be as stupid as my brother is," he said. "Or I might have to treat you the same way."

She was frightened now, she couldn't help it, not with cold pouring into her, chilling her bones. The wind was picking up again, the branches tossing. "Tell me where he is, Damon."

"At this moment? I don't know. Can't you stop thinking about him for an instant?"

"No!" She shuddered, hair lashing about her face again.

"And that's your final answer, today? Be very sure you want to play this game with me, Elena. The consequences are nothing to laugh about."

"I *am* sure." She had to stop him before he got to her again. "And you can't intimidate me, Damon, or haven't you noticed? The moment Stefan told me what you were, what you'd done, you lost any power you might have had over me. I *hate* you. You disgust me. And there's nothing you can do to me, not any more."

His face altered, the sensuousness twisting and freezing, becoming cruel and bitterly hard. He laughed, but this laugh went on and on. "Nothing?" he said. "I can do *anything* to you. You have no idea, Elena, of what I can do. But you'll learn."

He stepped back and the wind cut through Elena like a knife. Her vision seemed to be blurring—it was as if flecks of brightness filled the air in front of her eyes.

"Winter is coming, Elena," he said, and his voice was clear and chilling even over the howl of the wind. "An unforgiving season. Before it's over you'll have learned what I can and can't do. Before winter is over you'll have joined me. You'll be mine."

The swirling whiteness was blinding her and now even his voice was fading. She could no longer see the dark bulk of his figure. She hugged herself with her arms, head bent down, her whole body shaking. She whispered, "Stefan—"

"Oh, and one more thing," his voice came back. "You asked earlier about my brother. Don't bother looking for him, Elena. I killed him last night."

Her head jerked up, but there was nothing to see, only the dizzying whiteness, which burned her nose and cheeks and clogged her eyelashes. It was only then, as the fine grains settled on her skin that she realized what they were.

Snowflakes. It was snowing on the first of November. Overhead, the sun was gone.

Two

An unnatural twilight hung over the abandoned graveyard. Snow blurred Elena's eyes and the wind numbed her body as if she'd stepped into a current of ice water. Nevertheless, stubbornly, she did not turn around toward the modern cemetery and the road beyond it. As best she could judge, Wickery Bridge was straight in front of her. She headed for that.

The police had found Stefan's abandoned car by the Old Creek Road. That meant he'd left it somewhere between Drowning Creek and the woods. Elena stumbled on the overgrown path through the graveyard, but she kept moving, head down, arms hugging her light sweater to her. She had been born in Fell's Church, she had known this graveyard all her life, and she could find her way through it blind.

By the time she crossed the bridge her shivering had become painful. It wasn't snowing as hard now, but the wind was even worse. It cut through her clothes as if they were made of tissue paper, and took her breath away.

Stefan, she thought, and turned onto Old Creek Road, trudging northward. She didn't believe what Damon had said. If Stefan were dead she would *know*. He was alive, somewhere, and she had to find him. He could be anywhere out in this swirling whiteness, he could be hurt, freezing. Dimly, Elena sensed that she wasn't rational any longer. All her thoughts had narrowed down to one single idea. Stefan. Find Stefan.

It was getting harder to keep to the road. On her right were oak trees, on her left, the swift waters of Drowning Creek. She staggered and slowed. The wind didn't seem quite so bad anymore, but she did feel very tired. She needed to sit down and rest, just for a minute.

As she sank down beside the road she suddenly realized how silly she had been to go out searching for Stefan. Stefan would come to her. All she needed to do was sit here and wait. He was probably coming right now.

Elena shut her eyes and leaned her head against her drawn-up knees. She felt much warmer now. Her mind drifted and she saw Stefan, saw him smile at her. His arms around her were strong and secure and she relaxed against him, glad to let go of fear and tension. She was home, she was where she belonged. Stefan would never let anything hurt her.

But then instead of holding her, Stefan was shaking her. He was ruining the beautiful tranquility of her rest. She saw his face, pale and urgent, his green eyes dark with pain. She tried to tell him to be still, but he wouldn't listen. *Elena, get up*, he said, and she felt the compelling force of those green eyes willing her to do it. *Elena, get up now—*

"Elena, get up!" The voice was high and thin and frightened. "Come on, Elena! Get up! We can't carry you!"

Blinking, Elena brought a face into focus. "Bonnie," she said slowly. "What are you doing here?"

"Helping me look for you," said a second, lower voice, on Elena's other side. She turned slightly. Meredith's dark eyes, usually so ironic, were worried now, too. "Stand up, Elena, unless you want to become an Ice Princess for real."

There was snow all over her. Stiffly, Elena stood, leaning heavily on the two other girls. They walked her back to Meredith's car.

It should have been warmer inside the car, but Elena's nerve endings were coming back to life, telling her how cold she really was. Winter is an unforgiving season, she thought, as Meredith drove.

Aunt Judith was waiting inside, with blankets. "I knew if they found you you'd be half-frozen," she said in a determinedly cheerful voice as she reached for Elena. "Snow on the day after Halloween! I can hardly believe it. Where did you girls find her?"

"On the Old Creek Road, past the bridge," said Meredith.

Aunt Judith's thin face lost color. "Near the graveyard? Where the attacks were? Elena, how *could* you . . ." Her voice trailed off as she looked at Elena. "We won't say anything more about it right now," she said, trying to regain her cheerful manner. "Let's get you out of those wet clothes."

"I have to go back once I'm dry," said Elena. Her brain was working again and one thing was clear. She hadn't really seen Stefan out there; it had been a dream. Stefan was still missing.

"You have to do nothing of the kind," said Robert, Aunt Judith's fiancé. Elena had scarcely noticed him until then, standing quietly to one side. But his tone brooked no argument. "The police are looking for Stefan, you leave them to their job," he said.

"The police think he killed Mr. Tanner. But he didn't. You know that, don't you?" As Aunt Judith pulled her sodden outer sweater off, Elena looked from one face to another for help, but they were all the same. "You *know* he didn't do it," she repeated, almost desperately.

There was a silence. "Elena," Meredith said at last, "no one wants to think he did. But— well, it looks bad, his running away like this."

"He didn't run away. He didn't! He *didn't*—"

"Elena, hush," said Aunt Judith. "Don't get yourself worked up. I think you must be getting sick, it was so cold out there, and you only got a few hours of sleep last night . . ." She laid a hand on Elena's cheek.

"I'm not sick," she cried, pulling away. "And I'm not crazy, either, whatever you think. Stefan didn't run away and he didn't kill Mr. Tanner, and I don't care if none of you belives me . . ." She stopped, choking. Aunt Judith was fussing around her, hurrying her upstairs, and she let herself be hurried. But she wouldn't go to bed when Aunt Judith suggested she must be tired. Instead, she sat on the living room couch, by the fireplace, with blankets heaped around her. The phone rang all afternoon, and she heard Aunt Judith talking to friends, neighbors, the school. She assured all of them that Elena was fine. The—the tragedy last night had unsettled her a bit, that was all, and she seemed a little feverish. But she'd be good as new after a rest.

Meredith and Bonnie sat beside her. "Do you want to talk?" Meredith said in a low voice. Elena shook her head, staring into the fire. They were all against her. And Aunt Judith was wrong; she wasn't fine. She wouldn't be fine until Stefan was found.

Meredith and Bonnie and Aunt Judith and Robert tried to make conversation while they ate an early supper sitting by the fire. Elena couldn't eat and wouldn't talk. The only one who wasn't miserable was Elena's little sister Margaret. With four-year-old optimism she cuddled up to Elena and offered her some of her Halloween candy. Elena hugged her hard, face pressed into Margaret's white-blond hair for a moment. If Stefan could have called her or gotten a message to her he would have done it by now. Nothing in the world would have stopped him, unless he were badly hurt, or trapped somewhere, or . . .

She wouldn't let herself think about that last "or." Stefan was alive, he had to be alive. Damon was a liar.

But Stefan was in trouble, and she had to find him somehow. She worried about it all through the evening, desperately trying to come up with a plan. One thing was clear; she was on her own. She couldn't trust anyone.

It grew dark. Elena shifted on the couch and forced a yawn.

"I'm tired," she said quietly. "Maybe I am sick, after all. I think I'll go to bed."

Meredith was looking at her keenly. "I was just thinking, Miss Gilbert," she said, turning to Aunt Judith, "that maybe Bonnie and I should stay the night. To keep Elena company."

"What a good idea," said Aunt Judith, pleased. "As long as your parents don't mind, I'd be glad to have you."

"It's a long drive back to Herron. I think I'll stay, too," Robert said. "I can just stretch out on the couch here." Elena sat stonily, after looking once from the couch to the hall where the front door stood plainly in view. They'd planned this between them, or at least they were all in on it now. They were making sure she didn't leave the house.

When she emerged from the bathroom a little while later, wrapped in her red silk kimono, she found Meredith and Bonnie sitting on her bed.

"Well, hello, Rosencrantz and Guildenstern," she said bitterly.

Bonnie, who had been looking depressed, now looked alarmed. She glanced at Meredith doubtfully.

"She knows who we are. She means she thinks we're spies for her aunt," Meredith interpreted. "Elena, you should realize that isn't so. Can't you trust us at all?"

"I don't know. Can I?"

"Yes, because we're your *friends*." Before Elena could move Meredith jumped off the bed and shut the door. Then she turned to face Elena. "Now, for once in your life listen to me, you little idiot. It's true we don't know what to think about Stefan. But, don't you see, that's your own fault. Ever since you and he got together you've been shutting us out. Things have been happening that you haven't told us about. At least you haven't told us the whole story. But in spite of that, in spite of everything, we still trust you. We still care about you. We're still behind you, Elena, and we want to help. And if you can't see that, then you *are* an idiot."

Slowly, Elena looked from Meredith's dark, intense face to Bonnie's pale one. Bonnie nodded.

"It's true," she said, blinking hard as if to keep back tears. "Even if you don't like us, we still like *you*."

Elena felt her own eyes fill. "I'm sorry if I haven't been talking to you," she said. "I know you don't understand, and I can't even explain why I can't tell you anything. I just *can't*. But there's one thing I can tell you." She stepped back, wiping her cheeks, and looked at them earnestly. "No matter how bad the evidence against Stefan looks, *he didn't kill Mr. Tanner*. I know he didn't, because I know who did. And it's the same person who attacked Vickie, and the old man under the bridge."

Bonnie shook her head dazedly. Meredith said, "Why don't you tell the police?"

Elena's laugh was slightly hysterical. "I can't. It's not something they can deal with. And that's another thing I can't explain. You said you still trusted me; well, you'll just have to trust me about that."

Bonnie and Meredith looked at one another, then at the bedspread, where Elena's nervous fingers were picking a thread out of the embroidery. Finally Meredith said, "All right. What can we do to help?"

"I don't know. Nothing, unless . . ." Elena stopped and looked at Bonnie. "Unless," she said, in a changed voice, "you can help me find Stefan."

Bonnie's brown eyes were genuinely bewildered. "Me? But what can I do?" Then at Meredith's indrawn breath, she said, "Oh. *Oh.*"

"You knew where I was that day I went to the cemetery," said Elena. "And you even predicted Stefan's coming to school."

"I thought you didn't believe in all that psychic stuff," said Bonnie weakly.

"I've learned a thing or two since then. Anyway, I'm willing to believe *anything* if it'll help find Stefan. If there's any chance at all it will help."

Bonnie was hunching up, as if trying to make her already tiny form as small as possible. "Elena, you don't understand," she said wretchedly. "I'm not trained, it's not something I can control. And . . . and it's not a game, not anymore. The more you use those powers, the more they use *you.* Eventually, they can end up using you all the time, whether you want it or not. It's *dangerous.*"

Elena got up and walked to the cherrywood dresser, looking down at it without seeing it. At last she turned.

"You're right; it's not a game. And I believe you about how dangerous it can be. But it's not a game for Stefan, either. Bonnie, I think he's out there, somewhere, terribly hurt. And there's nobody to help him, nobody's even looking for him, except his enemies. He may be dying right now. He—he may even be . . ." Her throat closed. She bowed her head over the dresser and made herself take a deep breath, trying to steady herself. When she looked up she saw Meredith was looking at Bonnie.

Bonnie had straightened her shoulders, sitting up as tall as she could. Her chin was high and her mouth was set. And in her normally soft brown eyes a grim light shone as they met Elena's.

"We need a candle," was all she said.

The match rasped and threw sparks in the darkness, and then the candle flame burned strong and bright. It lent a golden glow to Bonnie's pale face as she bent over it.

"I'm going to need both of you to help me focus," she said. "Look into the flame and think about Stefan. Picture him in your mind. No matter what happens, keep on looking at the flame. And whatever you do, don't say anything."

Elena nodded, and then the only sound in the room was soft breathing. *Stefan*, thought Elena, gazing into the flame, trying to pour all her will into the thought. She created him in her mind, using all her senses, conjuring him to her. The roughness of his woolen sweater under her cheek, the smell of his leather jacket, the strength of his arms around her. Oh, Stefan . . .

Bonnie's lashes fluttered and her breathing quickened, like a sleeper having a bad dream. Elena resolutely kept her eyes on the flame, but when Bonnie broke the silence a chill went up her spine.

At first it was just a moan, the sound of someone in pain. Then, as Bonnie tossed her head, breath coming in short bursts, it became words.

"Alone . . ." she said, and stopped. Elena's nails bit into her hand. "Alone . . . in the dark," said Bonnie. Her voice was distant and tortured.

There was another silence, and then Bonnie began to speak quickly.

"It's so dark and cold. And I'm alone. There's something behind me . . . jagged and hard.

Rocks. They used to hurt—but not now. I'm numb now, from the cold. So cold . . ." Bonnie twisted, as if trying to get away from something, and then she laughed, a dreadful laugh almost like a sob. "That's—funny. I never thought I'd want to see the sun so much. But it's always dark here. And cold. Water up to my neck, like ice. That's funny, too. Water everywhere—and me dying of thirst. So thirsty . . . hurts . . ."

Elena felt something tighten around her heart. Bonnie was inside Stefan's thoughts, and who knew what she might discover there? *Stefan, tell us where you are,* she thought desperately. *Look around, tell me what you see.*

"Thirsty. I need . . . life?" Bonnie's voice was doubtful, as if not sure how to translate some concept. "I'm weak. He said I'll always be the weak one. He's strong . . . a killer. But that's what I am, too. I killed Katherine; maybe I deserve to die. Why not just let go . . ."

"No!" said Elena, before she could stop herself. "Stefan—"

"Elena!" Meredith cried sharply at the same time. But Bonnie's head fell forward, the flow of words cut off. Horrified, Elena realized what she had done.

"Bonnie, are you all right? Can you find him again? I didn't mean to . . ."

Bonnie's head lifted. Her eyes were open now, but they looked at neither the candle nor at Elena. They stared straight ahead, expressionless. When she spoke, her voice was distorted, and Elena's heart stopped. It wasn't Bonnie's voice, but it was a voice Elena recognized. She'd heard it coming from Bonnie's lips once before, in the graveyard.

"Elena," the voice said, "don't go to the bridge. It's death, Elena. Death is waiting there." Then Bonnie slumped bonelessly.

Elena grabbed her shoulders and shook. "Bonnie!" she almost screamed. "Bonnie!"

Look for another terrifying thriller from Nicholas Adams, bestselling author of Horror High.

I. O. U.

One

Midnight. There was no moon, and the stars were gone. Silence clung to her. For a heartbeat, Sharon did not know where she was. Then, as a chill wind ruffled her hair, she recognized the woods.

The nightmare was back again.

She looked around, feeling the panic began as a dull throb in her chest. The same dead trees, branches clawing for the skies: leafless, lifeless, but somehow malicious. Like skeletons with evil eyes, all watching her. The ground underfoot was hard and dry. Any grasses or flowers had died and withered long ago. All that were left were roots and stones, all cold, hard, and waiting for her to begin to run.

Sharon's heart began to pound, and she could feel the adrenaline pumping. Her breaths were short, forming trails of mist about her face. She wore only her nightdress, as always, and the air was cold and damp. Despite this, a thin trickle of sweat crawled down her back. She rubbed at it, feeling her hand go clammy at the touch. Her gaze darted about her, but nothing moved—yet.

This was the way that it always began. And it always ended the same way, with her—

A sound!

She twisted around, vainly trying to make out something, anything, in those disjointed trees. She tried to call out, but her throat wouldn't obey her mind. She could feel her heart speeding up, pounding. Her breath hissed in and out of her nostrils, the only thing she could now hear. Wildly, she darted her eyes all across the eerie landscape. Nothing.

Wavering, she took a step backward. Her ankle caught on a root, and she almost lost her balance. She looked down, but there was nothing to see. She could barely make out the white shape of her naked feet.

They were there.

Sharon knew it, even though she couldn't see them. They had arrived, and were there, in the woods, somewhere. The man, the dark man, with his brooding eyes and slow, steady tread. And . . . the other. The un-man, the shapeless *thing* that plucked at the edge of her mind and refused ever to be seen.

Backing up another step, something grabbed at her long, blonde hair. This time she found her voice, and screamed, pulling forward. The twigs from the tree jerked free from her hair, as she spun to face her attacker. Just a tree.

This time.

Again, she felt that they were watching her, waiting for her nerve to break. Waiting for her to run. But this time, she wouldn't do it. This time she would be strong. She wrapped her right arm about her chest, as if pulling a cloak over her flimsy clothing. The chill from the ground was numbing her toes. Wriggling them, she tried to fight off the cold. Slowly, hesitantly, feeling ahead with her extended left hand, she started to walk. She *would not* run! Not this time.

Her fingers touched something cold, clammy, and *alive*. With a start, she drew back. Nothing happened, but she could feel something icky on her fingertips. She peered ahead, and could make out some sort of fungus growth on a tree. She had put her hand into that. Ugh! Her fingers felt filthy, contaminated, but there was nowhere to wipe them except her filmy nightgown. She didn't want to do that, and get the gross stuff even closer to her body. What could she do?

She could feel their eyes, watching, waiting, looking for her reaction. Trying to stay rational, Sharon bent down in the darkness, feeling out with her itching left hand for something, anything. Her fingers closed on something hard and rounded. As she started to rub the fungus-stuff onto whatever it was, the object suddenly came to life, skittering away from her. With a scream, she shot back upright, her chest heaving. Without conscious thought, she pulled her left hand close, smearing her fingers onto the gown.

Terrific. She could sense the contaminated spot, where it touched her thigh. It made her skin crawl, just knowing it was there. And she could smell the stuff now, a rancid odor of decay, sickly, and growing stronger.

She took a step forward, but of course the smell moved with her. It was the stench of death, she knew, of something rotting, and she had touched it . . .

The icy caress of the breeze stirred at her again, slipping beneath her nightdress and brushing her skin. A shock passed up her body, and she shivered. It was impossible to get warm.

Unless she ran. And she wouldn't do that.

Something crawled across her foot. Something chittering, with dozens of tiny, fast-moving feet. She screamed, and tried to kick it away. Something else, wavering, hesitant, reached out to touch her other foot. She spun around, choking back tears, and bony fingers grabbed her hair. She'd backed into the grip of one of the trees! With a sob, she pulled herself free.

The scampering things in the darkness started to move again, and her skin crawled. Insects, bugs, all after her because she was warm and the only living thing in these woods.

Forgetting her resolve, Sharon turned and ran.

She tried to protect her face from the stinging blows of the branches and twigs. She could feel the lashing of these icy fingers, and she was getting scratched and bruised. She felt the trickling of blood now, mixing with the film of sweat. Her feet pounded across the uneven ground, stumbling over the rocks and roots that tried to grab at her and pull her down to the dead soil. Her breathing was short, hard, burning pants now, as she strove to fight down the terror welling up within.

Blindly, she dashed onward. She fought off the clutching branches, heedless of the scrapes she was getting. Her legs felt dozens of tiny scratches from the brambles and thorns. She knew she was filthy, bloody and soaked with perspiration. The twigs tore at the nightdress, dragging at it as she ran, ripping bits of fabric from her only protection. But she couldn't stop. Not now.

Her chest and lungs burned with every short, coughing breath she took. She could feel the punishment the soles of her feet were taking as she ran across the jagged stones and twisting roots. Arms flailing, she ran, the terror growing within her. She wanted to scream, but she had no breath to spare for that.

It was a hunt, she knew: her pursuers were in no rush. They wanted her exhausted, ready to break, before they closed in. But knowing it and being able to do anything to fight it were not the same thing. After all, she knew that this was a dream, but the terror and the lacerations felt very real indeed.

Finally, she could go on no more. For one last time, she stumbled, and now she fell. She couldn't even feel the extra pain as she crashed to the ground. She did manage to force one arm under her shaking body, and levered herself into a sitting position beneath a skeletal tree. The branches over her head felt the bars of a cage, and she knew that she was trapped.

Every breath she took burned clear down to her stomach, and she could never take in enough air. She brushed the long hairs from her eyes, and stared out into the darkness.

He was there, watching. Though there was no real light, she could see something burning redly in his eyes as he stared at her. It was the same man as always—tall, dark, with long, untidy hair flapping in the breeze. His skin was pale, his red eyes sunken. She took all of this in without thinking, because her eyes were drawn to the blade he held.

It wasn't a normal knife. It was more like a cake knife, with a narrow blade that flattened out, then came to a sharp point. Dimly, she knew she had seen something like this knife before, and that it was important. But she couldn't place it. Besides which, this wasn't the time for cold, analytical thought.

This was when she died.

A slow smile crossed the man's face, twisting it unevenly. He had caught her thought, could scent her panic and utter weariness. He took a step forward, and she tried to crawl away. But the tree behind her held her firm. The blade rose, ready.

If it was only death that she had to face, she would almost welcome it at this point. The panic had built to fever pitch, and she knew that dying of fright wasn't simply an expression. The thumping of her heart against her rib cage told her that it was almost ready to burst. But death was only the start of it . . .

Behind her killer, still hardly there, was the Unseen. It lurked, just on the edges of vision, shifting, hungering, waiting. It was the force behind the man, the predator waiting for its next victim to be delivered. It was ravenous, waiting to devour her, body and soul.

Death would be only the beginning of her agonies.

The knife rose, as the man stepped forward. She flung her hand out, a futile gesture she was unable to halt. He laughed, and grabbed at her wrist. She cried aloud with the pain as he forced her arm aside, exposing her chest. Then, in a frenzy of movement, he struck, plunging that glittering blade straight for her.

At the last second, she screamed.

And shot bolt-upright in her bed, panting, sweating, clutching the sheets about her for protection. Her eyes flew open into the darkness of her own room. She could see shapes and shadows of her precious, familiar life, in the gray light coming through the window. The canopy of her bed, overhead, more protective than the tree she had just died under. The warmth of the bedclothes she gripped tightly to herself. The—

Twin red spots burned in the shadows by the doorway.

He was here, in her room! He had escaped from her dream! He—

She fought down the terror that was bubbling up within herself, moving slightly to get a better view of the redness. Then she sighed with relief.

It was the light from her digital alarm, hitting her mirror on the far wall. There really wasn't anyone in the room with her at all. She was alone, and her parents were across the hall from her, and she was safe. Utterly, utterly safe. It had just been a dream.

Then the redness winked out.

Terror started to build up again in her. She could feel something in the room, something malevolent, something watching her, savoring the smell of her fear. She couldn't turn her head to see. If she didn't look, maybe, maybe she'd be wrong, and it wasn't there.

If the redness had been the alarm clock in the mirror, then why had it suddenly vanished?

Refusing to surrender to the childish urge to dive under the bedcovers and cry, she fought the tense muscles in her neck, slowly managing to twist her head about to look at the clock.

The front wasn't lit at all. Then, as she stared, the red numbers came back to life, blinking 12:00, over and over.

She let her breath out in one long rush. It had been a momentary power failure, nothing more. The figures flashed on and off now, demanding to taken care of, and she reached out a hesitant hand for her watch. She half expected something to reach out of the gloom and grab her, but nothing did. She glanced at the watchface, but could make nothing out. It was too dark. She switched on the bedside lamp, and quickly glanced all around her room. Everything was normal, just as it had been when she had turned off the light to go to sleep.

3:32 in the morning! She brushed her hair back and reached over, setting the alarm again. Then she took a drink of the water on her night-table. One last look around, to be certain that all was fine, then she reached for the light.

And hesitated. Maybe she'd be better off leaving it on for the last couple of hours of the night? Then she took a grip on her fears, and refused to revert to her childhood dread of the darkness. There was nothing there to harm her, nothing at all. It had just been a bad dream that she'd been having.

For the fourth time.

Fighting back her worries, she hastily switched off the light, and buried herself under the bedcovers again. Their warmth about her was comforting. But her nightdress stuck to her where she had been sweating, and she wriggled uncomfortably. She was exhausted, as if she'd really been running those terror-filled miles in the eerie forest. And her feet hurt. She rubbed at her left sole, trying to ease the cramping sensations. It didn't help much. And it felt rough, and sore. Almost as if she had been racing through woods in her bare feet. With a sigh of relief, she was just glad that there wasn't any blood or scratches on her body. Had there been, she just might have given in to the panic that lurked slightly over the threshold of her consciousness. She was afraid to return to sleep, in case the dream came back. Maybe she'd just stay awake until the morning . . . Slowly, without being aware of it, Sharon drifted into a dreamless slumber for the remainder of the night.